Fame and Fortune

or,

The Progress of Richard Hunter

by

Horatio Alger, Jr.

CHAPTER I.

A BOARDING-HOUSE IN BLEECKER STREET.

"Well, Fosdick, this is a little better than our old room in Mott Street," said Richard Hunter, looking complacently about him.

"You're right, Dick," said his friend. "This carpet's rather nicer than the ragged one Mrs. Mooney supplied us with. The beds are neat and comfortable, and I feel better satisfied, even if we do have to pay twice as much for it."

The room which yielded so much satisfaction to the two boys was on the fourth floor of a boarding-house in Bleecker Street. No doubt many of my young readers, who are accustomed to elegant homes, would think it very plain; but neither Richard nor his friend had been used to anything as good. They had been thrown upon their own exertions at an early age, and had a hard battle to fight with poverty and ignorance. Those of my readers who are familiar with Richard Hunter's experiences when he was "Ragged Dick," will easily understand what a great rise in the world it was for him to have a really respectable home. For years he had led a vagabond life about the streets, as a boot-black, sleeping in old wagons, or boxes, or wherever he could find a lodging gratis. It was only twelve months since a chance meeting with an intelligent boy caused him to form the resolution to grow up respectable. By diligent evening study with Henry Fosdick, whose advantages had been much greater than his own, assisted by a natural quickness and an unusual aptitude for learning, he had, in a year, learned to read and write well, and had, besides, made considerable progress in arithmetic. Still he would have found it difficult to obtain a situation if he had not been the means of saving from drowning the young child of Mr. James Rockwell, a wealthy merchant in business on Pearl Street, who at once, out of gratitude for the service rendered, engaged our hero in his employ at the unusual compensation, for a beginner, of ten dollars a week. His friend, Henry Fosdick, was in a hat store on Broadway, but thus far only received six dollars a week.

Feeling that it was time to change their quarters to a more respectable portion of the city, they one morning rang the bell of Mrs. Browning's boarding-house, on Bleecker Street.

They were shown into the parlor, and soon a tall lady, with flaxen ringlets and a thin face, came in.

"Well, young gentleman, what can I do for you?" she said, regarding them attentively.

"My friend and I are looking for a boarding-place," said Henry Fosdick. "Have you any rooms vacant?"

"What sort of a room would you like?" asked Mrs. Browning.

"We cannot afford to pay a high price. We should be satisfied with a small room."

"You will room together, I suppose?"

"Yes, ma'am."

1

"I have a room vacant on the third floor, quite a good-sized one, for which I should charge you seven dollars apiece. There is a room on the fourth floor, not so large, which you can have for five dollars each."

"I think we'll look at that," said Richard Hunter.

"Very well, then follow me."

Mrs. Browning preceded the boys to the fourth floor, where she opened the door of a neat room, provided with two single beds, a good-sized mirror, a bureau, a warm woollen carpet, a washstand, and an empty bookcase for books. There was a closet also, the door of which she opened, showing a row of pegs for clothing.

"How do you like it?" asked Fosdick, in a low voice, turning to his companion.

"It's bully," said Dick, in admiring accents.

I may as well say here, what the reader will find out as we proceed, that our hero, in spite of his advance in learning, had not got entirely rid of some street phrases, which he had caught from the companions with whom he had for years associated.

"Five dollars is rather a steep price," said Fosdick, in a low voice. "You know I don't get but six in all."

"I'll tell you what, Fosdick," said Dick; "it'll be ten dollars for the two of us. I'll pay six, and you shall pay four. That'll be fair,—won't it?"

"No, Dick, I ought to pay my half."

"You can make it up by helpin' me when I run against a snag, in my studies."

"You know as much as I do now, Dick."

"No, I don't. I haven't any more ideas of grammar than a broomstick. You know I called 'cat' a conjunction the other day. Now, you shall help me in grammar, for I'm blessed if I know whether I'm a noun or an adjective, and I'll pay a dollar towards your board."

"But, Dick, I'm willing to help you for nothing. It isn't fair to charge you a dollar a week for my help."

"Why isn't it? Aint I to get ten dollars a week, and shan't I have four dollars over, while you will only have two? I think I ought to give you one more, and then we'd be even."

"No, Dick; I wouldn't agree to that. If you insist upon it, we'll do as you propose; but, if ever I am able, I will make it up to you."

"Well, young gentleman, what have you decided?" asked Mrs. Browning.

"We'll take the room," said Dick, promptly.

"When do you wish to commence?"

"To-day. We'll come this evening."

"Very well. I suppose you can furnish me with references. You're in business, I suppose?"

"I am in Henderson's hat and cap store, No. —— Broadway," said Henry Fosdick.

"And I am going into Rockwell & Cooper's, on Pearl Street, next Monday," said Dick, with a sense of importance. He felt that this was very different from saying, "I black boots in Chatham Square."

"You look like good boys," said Mrs. Browning, "and I've no doubt you're honest; but I'm a widow, dependent on my boarders, and I have to be particular. Only last week a young man went off, owing me four weeks' board, and I don't suppose he'll ever show his face again. He got a good salary, too; but he spent most of it on cigars and billiards. Now, how can I be sure you will pay me your board regular?"

"We'll pay it every week in advance," said Dick, promptly. "Them's our best references," and he produced his bank-book, showing a deposit of over one hundred dollars to his credit in the savings bank, motioning at the same time to Fosdick to show his.

"You don't mean to say you've saved all that from your earnings?" said Mrs. Browning, surprised.

"Yes," said Dick, "and I might have saved more if I'd begun sooner."

"How long has it taken you to save it up?"

"About nine months. My friend hasn't saved so much, because his salary has been smaller."

"I won't require you to pay in advance," said Mrs. Browning, graciously. "I am sure I can trust you. Boys who have formed so good a habit of saving can be depended upon. I will get the room ready for you, and you may bring your trunks when you please. My hours are, breakfast at seven, lunch at half-past twelve, and dinner at six."

"We shan't be able to come to lunch," said Fosdick. "Our stores are too far off."

"Then I will make half a dollar difference with each of you, making nine dollars a week instead of ten."

The boys went downstairs, well pleased with the arrangement they had made. Dick insisted upon paying five dollars and a half of the joint weekly expense, leaving three and a half to Fosdick. This would leave the latter two dollars and a half out of his salary, while Dick would have left four and a half. With economy, both thought they could continue to lay up something.

There was one little embarrassment which suggested itself to the boys. Neither of them had a trunk, having been able to stow away all their wardrobe without difficulty in the drawers of the bureau with which their room in Mott Street was provided.

"Why are you like an elephant, Fosdick?" asked Dick, jocosely, as they emerged into the street.

"I don't know, I'm sure."

"Because you haven't got any trunk except what you carry round with you."

"We'll have to get trunks, or perhaps carpet-bags would do."

"No," said Dick, decisively, "it aint 'spectable to be without a trunk, and we're going to be 'spectable now."

"*Re*spectable, Dick."

"All right,—respectable, then. Let's go and buy each a trunk."

This advice seemed reasonable, and Fosdick made no objection. The boys succeeded in getting two decent trunks at three dollars apiece, and ordered them sent to their room in Mott Street. It must be remembered by my readers, who may regard the prices given as too low, that the events here recorded took place several years before the war, when one dollar was equal to two at the present day.

At the close of the afternoon Fosdick got away from the store an hour earlier, and the boys, preceded by an expressman bearing their trunks, went to their new home. They had just time to wash and comb their hair, when the bell rang for dinner, and they went down to the dining-room.

Nearly all the boarders were assembled, and were sitting around a long table spread with a variety of dishes. Mrs. Browning was a good manager, and was wise enough to set a table to which her boarders could not object.

"This way, if you please, young gentlemen," she said, pointing to two adjoining seats on the opposite side of the table.

Our hero, it must be confessed, felt a little awkward, not being used to the formality of a boarding-house, and feeling that the eyes of twenty boarders were upon him. His confusion was increased, when, after taking his seat, he saw sitting opposite him, a young man whose boots he remembered to have blacked only a week before. Observing Dick's look, Mrs. Browning proceeded to introduce him to the other.

"Mr. Clifton," she said, "let me introduce Mr. Hunter and his friend, Mr. Fosdick,—two new members of our family."

Dick bowed rather awkwardly, and the young man said, "Glad to make your acquaintance, Mr. Hunter. Your face looks quite familiar. I think I must have seen you before."

"I think I've seen *you* before," said Dick.

"It's strange I can't think where," said the young man, who had not the least idea that the well-dressed boy before him was the boot-black who had brushed his boots near the Park railings the Monday previous. Dick did not think proper to enlighten him. He was not ashamed of his past occupation; but it was past, and he wanted to be valued for what he might become, not for what he had been.

"Are you in business, Mr. Hunter?" inquired Mr. Clifton.

It sounded strange to our hero to be called Mr. Hunter; but he rather liked it. He felt that it sounded respectable.

"I am at Rockwell & Cooper's, on Pearl Street," said Dick.

"I know the place. It is a large firm."

Dick was glad to hear it, but did not say that he knew nothing about it.

The dinner was a good one, much better than the two boys were accustomed to get at the eating-houses which in times past they had frequented. Dick noticed carefully how the others did, and acquitted himself quite creditably, so that no one probably suspected that he had not always been used to as good a table.

When the boys rose from the table, Mrs. Browning said, "Won't you walk into the parlor, young gentlemen? We generally have a little music after dinner. Some of the young ladies are musical. Do either of you play?"

Dick said he sometimes played marbles; at which a young lady laughed, and Dick, catching the infection, laughed too.

"Miss Peyton, Mr. Hunter," introduced Mrs. Browning.

Miss Peyton made a sweeping courtesy, to which Dick responded by a bow, turning red with embarrassment.

"Don't you sing, Mr. Hunter?" asked the young lady.

"I aint much on warblin'," said Dick, forgetting for the moment where he was.

This droll answer, which Miss Peyton supposed to be intentionally funny, convulsed the young lady with merriment.

"Perhaps your friend sings?" she said.

Thereupon Fosdick was also introduced. To Dick's astonishment, he answered that he did a little. It was accordingly proposed that they should enter the next room, where there was a piano. The young lady played some well-known melodies, and Fosdick accompanied her with his voice, which proved to be quite sweet and melodious.

"You are quite an acquisition to our circle," said Miss Peyton, graciously. "Have you boarded in this neighborhood before?"

"No," said Fosdick; "at another part of the city."

He was afraid she would ask him in what street, but fortunately she forbore.

In about half an hour the boys went up to their own room, where they lighted the gas, and, opening their trunks, placed the contents in the bureau-drawers.

"Blessed if it don't seem strange," said Dick, "for a feller brought up as I have been to live in this style. I wonder what Miss Peyton would have said if she had known what I had been."

"You haven't any cause to be ashamed of it, Dick. It wasn't a very desirable business, but it was honest. Now you can do something better. You must adapt yourself to your new circumstances."

"So I mean to," said Dick. "I'm going in for respectability. When I get to be sixty years old, I'm goin' to wear gold spectacles and walk round this way, like the old gentlemen I see most every day on Wall Street."

Dick threw his head back, and began to walk round the room with a pompous step and an air of great importance.

"I hope we'll both rise, Dick; we've got well started now, and there've been other boys, worse off than we are, who have worked hard, and risen to Fame and Fortune."

"We can try," said Dick. "Now let us go out and have a walk."

"All right," said Fosdick.

They went downstairs, and out into the street. Accustomed to the lower part of the city, there was a novelty in the evening aspect of Broadway, with its shops and theatres glittering with light. They sauntered carelessly along, looking in at the shop-windows, feeling more and more pleased with their change of location. All at once Dick's attention was drawn to a gentleman accompanied by a boy of about his own size, who was walking a little in advance.

"Stop a minute," he said to Fosdick, and hurrying forward placed his hand on the boy's arm.

"How are you, Frank?" he said.

Frank Whitney, for it was he, turned in some surprise and looked at Dick, but did not at first recognize in the neat, well-dressed boy of fifteen the ragged boot-black he had encountered a year before.

"I don't think I remember you," he said, surveying Dick with a puzzled expression.

"Perhaps you'd remember me better if I had on my Washington coat and Napoleon pants," said our hero, with a smile. He felt rather pleased to find he was not recognized, since it was a compliment to his improved appearance.

"What!" exclaimed Frank, his face lighting up with pleasure, "is it possible that you are—"

"Richard Hunter, at your service," said our hero; "but when you knew me I was Ragged Dick."

CHAPTER II.

INTRODUCTION TO MERCANTILE LIFE.

Frank Whitney was indeed surprised to find the ragged boot-black of a year before so wonderfully changed. He grasped Dick's hand, and shook it heartily.

"Uncle," he said, "this is Dick. Isn't he changed?"

"It is a change I am glad to see," said Mr. Whitney, also extending his hand; "for it appears to be a change for the better. And who is this other young man?"

"This is my private tutor," said Dick, presenting Fosdick,—"Professor Fosdick. He's been teachin' me every evenin' for most a year. His terms is very reasonable. If it hadn't been for him, I never should have reached my present high position in literature and science."

"I am glad to make your acquaintance, *Professor* Fosdick," said Frank, laughing. "May I inquire whether my friend Dick owes his elegant system of pronunciation to your instructions?"

"Dick can speak more correctly when he pleases," said Fosdick; "but sometimes he falls back into his old way. He understands the common English branches very well."

"Then he must have worked hard; for when I first met him a year ago, he was—"

"As ignorant as a horse," interrupted Dick. "It was you that first made me ambitious, Frank. I wanted to be like you, and grow up 'spectable."

"*R*espectable, Dick," suggested Fosdick.

"Yes, that's what I mean. I didn't always want to be a boot-black, so I worked hard, and with the help of Professor Fosdick, I've got up a little way. But I'm goin' to climb higher."

"I am very glad to hear it, my young friend," said Mr. Whitney. "It is always pleasant to see a young man fighting his way upward. In this free country there is

6

every inducement for effort, however unpromising may be the early circumstances in which one is placed. But, young gentlemen, as my nephew would be glad to speak further with you, I propose that we adjourn from the sidewalk to the St. Nicholas Hotel, where I am at present stopping."

"Yes, Dick," said Frank, "you and Professor Fosdick must spend the evening with me. I was intending to visit some place of amusement, but would much prefer a visit from you."

Dick and Fosdick readily accepted this invitation, and turned in the direction of the St. Nicholas, which is situated on Broadway, below Bleecker Street.

"By the way, Dick, where are your Washington coat and Napoleon pants now?"

"They were stolen from my room," said Dick, "by somebody that wanted to appear on Broadway dressed in tip-top style, and hadn't got money enough to pay for a suit."

"Perhaps it was some agent of Barnum who desired to secure the valuable relics," suggested Frank.

"By gracious!" said Dick, suddenly, "there they are now. It's the first time I've seen 'em since they was stolen."

He pointed to a boy, of about his own size, who was coming up Broadway. He was attired in the well-remembered coat and pants; but, alas! time had not spared them. The solitary remaining coat-tail was torn in many places; of one sleeve but a fragment remained; grease and dirt nearly obliterated the original color; and it was a melancholy vestige of what it had been once. As for the pantaloons, they were a complete wreck. When Dick had possessed them they were well ventilated; but they were now ventilated so much more thoroughly that, as Dick said afterwards, "a feller would be warmer without any."

"That's Micky Maguire," said Dick; "a partic'lar friend of mine, that had such a great 'fection for me that he stole my clothes to remember me by."

"Perhaps," said Fosdick, "it was on account of his great respect for General Washington and the Emperor Napoleon."

"What would the great Washington say if he could see his coat now?" said Frank.

"When I wore it," said Dick, "I was sorry he was so great, 'cause it prevented his clothes fitting me."

It may be necessary to explain to those who are unacquainted with Dick's earlier adventures, that the clothes in which he was originally introduced were jocosely referred to by him as gifts from the illustrious personages whose names have been mentioned.

Micky Maguire did not at first recognize Dick. When he did so, he suddenly shambled down Prince Street, fearful, perhaps, that the stolen clothes would be reclaimed.

They had now reached the St. Nicholas, and entered. Mr. Whitney led the way up to his apartment, and then, having a business engagement with a gentleman below, he descended to the reading-room, leaving the boys alone. Left to themselves, they talked freely. Dick related fully the different steps in his education, with which some of our readers are already familiar, and received hearty congratulations from Frank, and earnest encouragement to persevere.

"I wish you were going to be in the city, Frank," said Dick.

"So I shall be soon," said Frank.

Dick's face lighted up with pleasure.

"That's bully," said he, enthusiastically. "How soon are you comin'?"

"I am hoping to enter Columbia College next commencement. I suppose my time will be a good deal taken up with study, but I shall always find time for you and Fosdick. I hope you both will call upon me."

Both boys readily accepted the invitation in advance, and Dick promised to write to Frank at his boarding-school in Connecticut. At about half past ten, the two boys left the St. Nicholas, and went back to their boarding-house.

After a comfortable night's sleep, they got up punctually to the seven o'clock breakfast. It consisted of beefsteak, hot biscuit, potatoes, and very good coffee. Dick and Fosdick did justice to the separate viands, and congratulated themselves upon the superiority of their present fare to that which they had been accustomed to obtain at the restaurants.

Breakfast over, Fosdick set out for the hat and cap store in which he was employed, and Dick for Rockwell & Cooper's on Pearl Street. It must be confessed that he felt a little bashful as he stood in front of the large warehouse, and surveyed the sign. He began to feel some apprehensions that he would not be found competent for his post. It seemed such a rise from the streets to be employed in such an imposing building. But Dick did not long permit timidity to stand in his way. He entered the large apartment on the first floor, which he found chiefly used for storing large boxes and cases of goods. There was a counting-room and office, occupying one corner, partitioned off from the rest of the department. Dick could see a young man through the glass partition sitting at a desk; and, opening the door, he entered. He wished it had been Mr. Rockwell, for it would have saved him from introducing himself; but of course it was too early for that gentleman to appear.

"What is your business?" inquired the book-keeper, for it was he.

"I've come to work," said Dick, shortly, for somehow he did not take much of a fancy to the book-keeper, whose tone was rather supercilious.

"Oh, you've come to work, have you?"

"Yes, I have," said Dick, independently.

"I don't think we shall need your valuable services," said the book-keeper, with something of a sneer. The truth was, that Mr. Rockwell had neglected to mention that he had engaged Dick.

Dick, though a little inclined to be bashful when he entered, had quite got over that feeling now. He didn't intend to be intimidated or driven away by the man before him. There was only one doubt in his mind. This might be Mr. Cooper, the second member of the firm, although he did not think it at all probable. So he ventured this question, "Is Mr. Rockwell or Mr. Cooper in?"

"They're never here at this hour."

"So I supposed," said Dick, coolly.

He sat down in an arm-chair, and took up the morning paper.

The book-keeper was decidedly provoked by his coolness. He felt that he had not impressed Dick with his dignity or authority, and this made him angry.

"Bring that paper to me, young man," he said; "I want to consult it."

"Very good," said Dick; "you can come and get it."

"I can't compliment you on your good manners," said the other.

"Good manners don't seem to be fashionable here," said Dick, composedly.

Apparently the book-keeper did not want the paper very particularly, as he did not take the trouble to get up for it. Dick therefore resumed his reading, and the other dug his pen spitefully into the paper, wishing, but not quite daring, to order Dick out of the counting-room, as it might be possible that he had come by appointment.

"Did you come to see Mr. Rockwell?" he asked, at length, looking up from his writing.

"Yes," said Dick.

"Did he tell you to come?"

"Yes."

"What was that you said about coming to work?"

"I said I had come here to work."

"Who engaged you?"

"Mr. Rockwell."

"Oh, indeed! And how much are you to receive for your valuable services?"

"You are very polite to call my services valuable," said Dick. "I hope they will be."

"You haven't answered my question."

"I have no objection, I'm sure. I'm to get ten dollars a week."

"Ten dollars a week!" echoed the book-keeper, with a scornful laugh. "Do you expect you will earn that?"

"No, I don't," said Dick, frankly.

"You don't!" returned the other, doubtfully. "Well, you're more modest than I thought for. Then why are you to get so much?"

"Perhaps Mr. Rockwell will tell you," said Dick, "if you tell him you're very particular to know, and will lose a night's rest if you don't find out."

"I wouldn't give you a dollar a week."

"Then I'm glad I aint goin' to work for you."

"I don't believe your story at all. I don't think Mr. Rockwell would be such a fool as to overpay you so much."

"P'r'aps I shouldn't be the only one in the establishment that is overpaid," observed Dick.

"Do you mean me, you young rascal?" demanded the book-keeper, now very angry.

"Don't call names. It isn't polite."

"I demand an answer. Do you mean to say that I am overpaid?"

"Well," said Dick, deliberately, "if you're paid anything for bein' polite, I should think you was overpaid considerable."

There is no knowing how long this skirmishing would have continued, if Mr. Rockwell himself had not just then entered the counting-room. Dick rose respectfully at his entrance, and the merchant, recognizing him at once, advanced smiling and gave him a cordial welcome.

"I am glad to see you, my boy," he said. "So you didn't forget the appointment. How long have you been here?"

"Half an hour, sir."

"I am here unusually early this morning. I came purposely to see you, and introduce you to those with whom you will labor. Mr. Gilbert, this is a young man who is going to enter our establishment. His name is Richard Hunter. Mr. Gilbert, Richard, is our book-keeper."

Mr. Gilbert nodded slightly, not a little surprised at his employer's cordiality to the new boy.

"So the fellow was right, after all," he thought. "But it can't be possible he is to receive ten dollars a week."

"Come out into the ware-room, and I will show you about," continued Mr. Rockwell. "How do you think you shall like business, Richard?"

Dick was on the point of saying "Bully," but checked himself just in time, and said instead, "Very much indeed, sir."

"I hope you will. If you do well you may depend upon promotion. I shall not forget under what a heavy obligation I am to you, my brave boy."

What would the book-keeper have said, if he had heard this?

"How is the little boy, sir?" asked Dick.

"Very well, indeed. He does not appear even to have taken cold, as might have been expected from his exposure, and remaining in wet clothes for some time."

"I am glad to hear that he is well, sir."

"You must come up and see him for yourself, Richard," said Mr. Rockwell, in a friendly manner. "I have no doubt you will become good friends very soon. Besides, my wife is anxious to see and thank the preserver of her boy."

"I shall be very glad indeed to come, sir."

"I live at No. —— Madison Avenue. Come to-morrow evening, if you have no engagement."

"Thank you, sir."

Mr. Rockwell now introduced Dick to his head clerk with a few words, stating that he was a lad in whose welfare he took a deep interest, and he would be glad to have him induct him into his duties, and regard with indulgence any mistakes which he might at first make through ignorance.

The head clerk was a pleasant-looking man, of middle age, named Murdock; very different in his manners and bearing from Mr. Gilbert, the book-keeper.

"Yes, sir," he said, "I will take the young man under my charge; he looks bright and sharp enough, and I hope we may make a business man of him in course of time."

That was what Dick liked. His heart always opened to kindness, but harshness always made him defiant.

"I'll try to make you as little trouble as possible, sir," he said. "I may make mistakes at first, but I'm willin' to work, and I want to work my way up."

"That's right, my boy," said Mr. Murdock. "Let that be your determination, and I am sure you will succeed."

"Before Mr. Murdock begins to instruct you in your duties," said Mr. Rockwell, "you may go to the post-office, and see if there are any letters for us. Our box is No. 5,670."

"All right, sir," said Dick; and he took his hat at once and started.

He reached Chatham Square, turned into Printing House Square, and just at the corner of Spruce and Nassau Streets, close by the Tribune Office, he saw the familiar face and figure of Johnny Nolan, one of his old associates when he was a boot-black.

"How are you, Johnny?" he said.

"Is that you, Dick?" asked Johnny, turning round. "Where's your box and brush?"

"At home."

"You haven't give up business,—have you?"

"I've just gone into business, Johnny."

"I mean you aint give up blackin' boots,—have you?"

"All except my own, Johnny. Aint that a good shine?" and Dick displayed his boot with something of his old professional pride.

"What you up to now, Dick? You're dressed like a swell."

"Oh," said Dick, "I've retired from shines on a fortun', and embarked my capital in mercantile pursuits. I'm in a store on Pearl Street."

"What store?"

"Rockwell & Cooper's."

"How'd you get there?"

"They wanted a partner with a large capital, and so they took me," said Dick. "We're goin' to do a smashin' business. We mean to send off a ship to Europe every day, besides what we send to other places, and expect to make no end of stamps."

"What's the use of gassin', Dick? Tell a feller now."

"Honor bright, then, Johnny, I've got a place at ten dollars a week, and I'm goin' to be 'spectable. Why don't you turn over a new leaf, and try to get up in the world?"

"I aint lucky, Dick. I don't half the time make enough to live on. If it wasn't for the Newsboys' Lodgin' House, I don't know what I'd do. I need a new brush and box of blacking, but I aint got money enough to buy one."

"Then, Johnny, I'll help you this once. Here's fifty cents; I'll give it to you. Now, if you're smart you can make a dollar a day easy, and save up part of it. You ought to be more enterprisin', Johnny. There's a gentleman wants a shine now."

Johnny hitched up his trousers, put the fifty cents in his mouth, having no pocket unprovided with holes, and proffered his services to the gentleman indicated, with success. Dick left him at work, and kept on his way down Nassau Street.

"A year ago," he thought, "I was just like Johnny, dressed in rags, and livin' as I could. If it hadn't been for my meetin' with Frank, I'd been just the same to day, most likely. Now I've got a good place, and some money in the bank, besides 'ristocratic friends who invite me to come and see them. Blessed if I aint afraid I'm dreamin' it all, like the man that dreamed he was in a palace, and woke up to find himself in a pigpen."

CHAPTER III.

AT THE POST-OFFICE.

The New York Post-Office is built of brick, and was formerly a church. It is a shabby building, and quite unworthy of so large and important a city. Of course Dick was quite familiar with its general appearance; but as his correspondence had been very limited, he had never had occasion to ask for letters.

There were several letters in Box 5,670. Dick secured these, and, turning round to go out, his attention was drawn to a young gentleman of about his own age, who, from his consequential air, appeared to feel his own importance in no slight degree. He recognized him at once as Roswell Crawford, a boy who had applied unsuccessfully for the place which Fosdick obtained in Henderson's hat and cap store.

Roswell recognized Dick at the same time, and perceiving that our hero was well-dressed, concluded to speak to him, though he regarded Dick as infinitely beneath himself in the social scale, on account of his former employment. He might not have been so condescending, but he was curious to learn what Dick was about.

"I haven't seen you for some time," he said, in a patronizing tone.

"No," said Dick, "and I haven't seen you for some time either, which is a very curious coincidence."

"How's boot-blacking, now?" inquired Roswell, with something of a sneer.

"Tip-top," said Dick, not at all disturbed by Roswell's manner. "I do it wholesale now, and have been obliged to hire a large building on Pearl Street to transact my business in. You see them letters? They're all from wholesale customers."

"I congratulate you on your success," said Roswell, in the same disagreeable manner. "Of course that's all humbug. I suppose you've got a place."

"Yes," said Dick.

"Who are you with?"

"Rockwell & Cooper, on Pearl Street."

"How did you get it?" asked Roswell, appearing surprised. "Did they know you had been a boot-black?"

"Of course they did."

"I shouldn't think that they would have taken you."

"Why not?"

"There are not many firms that would hire a boot-black, when they could get plenty of boys from nice families."

"Perhaps they might have secured your services if they had applied," said Dick, good-humoredly.

"I've got a place," said Roswell, in rather an important manner. "I'm very glad I didn't go into Henderson's hat and cap store. I've got a better situation."

"Have you?" said Dick. "I'm glad to hear it. I'm always happy to hear that my friends are risin' in the world."

"You needn't class me among your friends," said Roswell, superciliously.

"No, I won't," said Dick. "I'm goin' to be particular about my associates, now that I'm gettin' up in the world."

"Do you mean to insult me?" demanded Roswell, haughtily.

"No," said Dick. "I wouldn't on any account. I should be afraid you'd want me to fight a duel, and that wouldn't be convenient, for I haven't made my will, and I'm afraid my heirs would quarrel over my extensive property."

"How much do you get a week?" asked Roswell, thinking it best to change the subject.

"Ten dollars," said Dick.

"Ten dollars!" ejaculated Roswell. "That's a pretty large story."

"You needn't believe it if you don't want to," said Dick. "That won't make any difference to me as long as they pay me reg'lar."

"Ten dollars! Why, I never heard of such a thing," exclaimed Roswell, who only received four dollars a week himself, and thought he was doing well.

"Do you think I'd give up a loocrative business for less?" asked Dick. "How much do you get?"

"That's my business," said Roswell, who, for reasons that may be guessed, didn't care to mention the price for which he was working. Judging Dick by himself, he thought it would give him a chance to exult over him.

"I suppose it is," said Dick; "but as you was so partic'lar to find out how much I got, I thought I'd inquire."

"You're trying to deceive me; I don't believe you get more than three dollars a week."

"Don't you? Is that what you get?"

"I get a great deal more."

"I'm happy to hear it."

"I can find out how much you get, if I want to."

"You've found out already."

"I know what you say, but I've got a cousin in Rockwell & Cooper's."

"Have you?" asked Dick, a little surprised. "Who is it?"

"It is the book-keeper."

"Mr. Gilbert?"

"Yes; he has been there five years. I'll ask him about it."

"You'd better, as you're so anxious to find out. Mr. Gilbert is a friend of mine. He spoke only this morning of my valooable services."

Roswell looked incredulous. In fact he did not understand Dick at all; nor could he comprehend his imperturbable good-humor. There were several things that he had said which would have offended most boys; but Dick met them with a careless good-humor, and an evident indifference to Roswell's good opinion, which piqued and provoked that young man.

It must not be supposed that while this conversation was going on the boys were standing in the post-office. Dick understood his duty to his employers too well to delay unnecessarily while on an errand, especially when he was sent to get letters, some of which might be of an important and urgent nature.

The two boys had been walking up Nassau Street together, and they had now reached Printing House Square.

"There are some of your old friends," said Roswell, pointing to a group of ragged boot-blacks, who were on the alert for customers, crying to each passer, "Shine yer boots?"

"Yes," said Dick, "I know them all."

"No doubt," sneered Roswell. "They're friends to be proud of."

"I'm glad you think so," said Dick. "They're a rough set," he continued, more earnestly; "but there's one of them, at least, that's ten times better than you or I."

"Speak for yourself, if you please," said Roswell, haughtily.

"I'm speakin' for both of us," said Dick. "There's one boy there, only twelve years old, that's supported his sick mother and sister for more'n a year, and that's more good than ever you or I did.—How are you, Tom?" he said, nodding to the boy of whom he had spoken.

"Tip-top, Dick," said a bright-looking boy, who kept as clean as his avocation would permit. "Have you given up business?"

"Yes, Tom. I'll tell you about it some other time. I must get back to Pearl Street with these letters. How's your mother?"

"She aint much better, Dick."

"Buy her some oranges. They'll do her good," and Dick slipped half a dollar into Tom's hand.

"Thank you, Dick. She'll like them, I know, but you oughtn't to give so much."

"What's half a dollar to a man of my fortune?" said Dick. "Take care of yourself, Tom. I must hurry back to the store."

Roswell was already gone. His pride would not permit him to stand by while Dick was conversing with a boot-black. He felt that his position would be compromised. As for Dick, he was so well dressed that nobody would know that he had ever been in that business. The fact is, Roswell, like a great many other people, was troubled with a large share of pride, though it might have puzzled himself to explain what he had to be proud of. Had Dick been at all like him he would have shunned all his former acquaintances, and taken every precaution against having it discovered that he had ever occupied a similar position. But Dick was above such meanness. He could see that Tom, for instance, was far superior in all that constituted manliness to Roswell Crawford, and, boot-black though he was, he prepared to recognize him as a friend.

When Dick reached the store, he did not immediately see Mr. Rockwell.

He accordingly entered the counting-room where Gilbert, the book-keeper, was seated at a desk.

"Here are the letters, Mr. Gilbert," said Dick.

"Lay them down," said the book-keeper, sourly. "You've been gone long enough. How many did you drop on the way?"

"I didn't know I was expected to drop any," said Dick. "If I had been told to do so, I would have obeyed orders cheerfully."

Mr. Gilbert was about to remark that Dick was an impudent young rascal, when the sudden entrance of Mr. Rockwell compelled him to suppress the observation, and he was obliged to be content with muttering it to himself.

"Back already, Richard?" said his employer, pleasantly. "Where are the letters?"

"Here, sir," said Dick.

"Very well, you may go to Mr. Murdock, and see what he can find for you to do."

Mr. Rockwell sat down to read his letters, and Dick went as directed to the head clerk.

"Mr. Rockwell sent me to you, Mr. Murdock," he said. "He says you will find something for me to do."

"Oh, yes, we'll keep you busy," said the head clerk, with a manner very different from that of the book-keeper. "At present, however, your duties will be of rather a miscellaneous character. We shall want you partly for an entry clerk, and partly to run to the post-office, bank, and so forth."

"All right, sir," said Dick. "I'm ready to do anything that is required of me. I want to make myself useful."

"That's the right way to feel, my young friend. Some boys are so big-feeling and put on so many airs, that you'd think they were partners in the business, instead of beginning at the lowest round of the ladder. A while ago Mr. Gilbert brought round a cousin of his, about your age, that he wanted to get in here; but the young gentleman was altogether too lofty to suit me, so we didn't take him."

"Was the boy's name Roswell Crawford?"

"Yes; do you know him?"

"Not much. He thinks I'm too far beneath him for him to associate with, but he was kind enough to walk up Nassau Street with me this morning, just to encourage me a little."

"That was kind in him, certainly," said the head clerk, smiling. "Unless I am very much mistaken, you will be able to get along without his patronage."

"I hope so," said Dick.

The rest of the day Dick was kept busy in various ways. He took hold with a will, and showed himself so efficient that he made a favorable impression upon every one in the establishment, except the book-keeper. For some reason or other Mr.

Gilbert did not like Dick, and was determined to oust him from his situation if an opportunity should offer.

CHAPTER IV.

LIFE AT THE BOARDING-HOUSE.

Dick found his new quarters in Bleecker Street very comfortable. His room was kept in neat order, which was more than could be said of his former home in Mott Street. There once a fortnight was thought sufficient to change the sheets, while both boys were expected to use the same towel, and make that last a week. Indeed, Mrs. Mooney would have considered the boys "mighty particular" if they had objected to such an arrangement. Mrs. Browning, fortunately, was very different, and Dick found nothing to complain of either in his chamber or in the board which was furnished.

Dick had felt rather awkward on his first appearance at the table, but he was beginning to feel more at his ease. It was rather remarkable, considering his past life, how readily he adapted himself to an experience so different. He left the store at five o'clock, and got to his boarding-house in time to get ready for dinner. Dick had now got to be quite particular about his appearance. He washed his face and hands thoroughly, and brushed his hair carefully, before appearing at the table.

Miss Peyton, the lively young lady who has already been mentioned in the first chapter, sat near the boys, and evidently was quite prepossessed in their favor. Both had bright and attractive faces, though Dick would undoubtedly be considered the handsomest. He had a fresh color which spoke of good health, and was well-formed and strong. Henry Fosdick was more delicate in appearance; his face was thinner, and rather pale. It was clear that he was not as well able to fight his way through life as Dick. But there was something pleasant and attractive in his quiet sedateness, as well as in the frank honesty and humor that could be read in the glance of our friend Dick.

"Won't you and your friend stop a little while and sing?" asked Miss Peyton, addressing Henry Fosdick on the evening of the second day of Dick's business career.

Fosdick hesitated.

"My friend has an engagement this evening," he said.

"I suppose I may not ask where," said she.

"I am invited to spend the evening with some friends on Madison Avenue," said Dick.

"Indeed?" said Miss Peyton, surprised. "I wasn't aware you had such fashionable friends, or I couldn't have expected to retain you."

"All my friends are not as fashionable," said Dick, wondering what the young lady would say if she could see his late fellow-lodgers at Mrs. Mooney's, on Mott Street.

"If I can't hope to keep you this evening, you must promise to stay awhile to-morrow evening. I hope to have the pleasure of hearing you sing, Mr. Hunter."

"When I give a concert," said Dick, "I'll be sure to let you in gratooitous."

"Thank you," said Miss Peyton. "I shall remind you of it. I hope that time will come very soon."

"Just as soon as I can engage the Academy of Music on reasonable terms."

"You'd better try first in the parlor here. We'll take up a contribution, to pay you for your exertions."

"Thank you," said Dick. "You're very kind, as the man said to the judge when he asked him when it would be perfectly agreeable for him to be hung."

Miss Peyton laughed at this remark, and Dick went upstairs to get ready for his visit to Madison Avenue.

Our hero felt a little bashful about this visit. He was afraid that he would do or say something that was improper, or that something would slip out which would betray his vagabond life of the streets.

"I wish you was going with me, Fosdick," he said.

"You'll get along well enough alone, Dick. Don't be afraid."

"You see I aint used to society, Fosdick."

"Nor I either."

"But it seems to come natural to you. I'm always makin' some blunder."

"You'll get over that in time, Dick. It's because you have so much fun in you. I am more sober. Miss Peyton seems very much amused by your odd remarks."

"I have to talk so; I can't think of anything else to say."

"There's one thing, Dick, we mustn't give up at any rate."

"What's that?"

"Studying. We don't either of us know as much as we ought to."

"That's so."

"You can see how much good studying has done for you so far. If it hadn't been for that, you wouldn't have been able to go into Mr. Rockwell's employment."

"That's true enough, Fosdick. I'm afraid I don't know enough now."

"You know enough to get along very well for the present, but you want to rise."

"You're right. When I get to be old and infirm I don't want to be an errand-boy."

"Nor I either. So, Dick, I think we had better make up our minds to study an hour or an hour and a half every evening. Of course, you can't begin this evening, but there are very few when you can't find the time."

"I'll send a circ'lar to my numerous friends on Fifth Avenue and Madison, tellin' 'em how much I'm obliged for their kind invitations, but the claims of literatoor and science can't be neglected."

"Do you know, Dick, I think it might be well for us to begin French?"

"I wonder what Johnny Nolan would say if I should inquire after his health in the polly-voo language?"

17

"It wouldn't be the first time you have astonished him."

"Well, Fosdick, I'm in for it if you think it's best. Now tell me what necktie I shall wear?"

Dick displayed two. One was bright red with large figures, which he had bought soon after he began to board in Mott Street. The other was a plain black.

"You'd better wear the black one, Dick," said Fosdick, whose taste was simpler and better than his friend's.

"It seems to me it don't look handsome enough," said Dick, whose taste had not yet been formed, and was influenced by the Bowery style of dress.

"It's more modest, and that is all the better."

"All right. I suppose you know best. Before I get ready I must give a new shine to my boots. I'm going to make them shine so you can see your face in them."

"Better let me do that for you, Dick. I can do it while you're dressing, and that will save time."

"No, Fosdick, I was longer in the business than you, and none of the boys could beat me on shines."

"I don't know but you're right, Dick. I freely yield the palm to you in that."

Dick stripped off his coat and vest and went to work with a will. He had never worked so hard for one of his old customers.

"I'm goin' to give it a twenty-five cent shine," he said.

Just then a knock was heard at the chamber-door.

"Come in!" said Dick, pausing a moment in his labors.

Mr. Clifton, a fellow-boarder, entered with a cigar in his mouth.

"Holloa," said he, "what's up? Going to the theatre, Hunter?"

"No," said Dick. "I'm goin' out to spend the evening with some friends up in Madison Avenue."

"So I heard you say at the table, but I thought you were joking."

"No," said Dick; "it's a fact."

"Seems to me you handle the brush pretty skilfully," remarked Mr. Clifton. "I should almost think you had served a regular apprenticeship at it."

"So I have," answered Dick. "Didn't you ever see me when I blacked boots on Chatham Square?"

"Good joke!" said the young man, who was far from supposing that Dick was in earnest. "Oh, yes, of course I've seen you often! Did you make money at it?"

"I retired on a fortun'," said Dick, "and now I've invested my capital in mercantile pursuits. There," and he took up one boot, and showed it to his visitor, "did you ever see a better shine than that?"

"No, I didn't, that's a fact," said Clifton, admiringly. "You beat the young rascal I employ all hollow. I say, Hunter, if you ever go into the 'shine' business again, I'll be a regular customer of yours."

"He little thinks I've blacked his boots before now," thought Dick.

"All right," said he, aloud. "When a commercial crisis comes, and I fail in business, I think I'll remember your encouragin' offer, and remind you of it."

"Have a cigar either of you?" asked Clifton, drawing out a case. "Excuse my not offering it before."

"No, thank you," said Fosdick.

"Don't smoke, eh? Won't you have one, Hunter?"

"No, thank you. Fosdick is my guardian, and he don't allow it."

"So you're a good boy. Well, I wish you a pleasant evening," and Clifton sauntered out to find some other companion.

"He wouldn't believe I'd been a boot-black," said Dick, "even after I told him. I knew he wouldn't, or I wouldn't have said so. Is my hair parted straight?"

"Yes, it's all right."

"How's my cravat?"

"It'll do. You're getting to be quite a dandy, Dick."

"I want to look respectable; got it right that time. When I visit Turkey I want to look as the turkeys do. Won't you go with me,—as far as the door, I mean?"

"Yes, if you're going to walk."

"I'd rather. I feel kind of nervous, and perhaps I'll walk it off."

The two boys got their caps, and walked up Broadway on the west side. The lights were already lit, and the shop windows made a brilliant display. At intervals places of amusement opened wide their hospitable portals, and large placards presented tempting invitations to enter.

They reached Union Square, and, traversing it, again walked up Broadway to Madison Park. At the upper end of this park commences the beautiful avenue which bears the same name. Only about half a dozen blocks now required to be passed, when the boys found themselves opposite a residence with a very imposing front.

"This is the place," said Dick. "I wish you were going in with me."

"I hope you will have a pleasant time, Dick. Good-by till I see you again."

Dick felt a little nervous, but he summoned up all his courage, and, ascending the broad marble steps, rang the bell.

CHAPTER V.

DICK RECEIVES TWO VALUABLE PRESENTS.

At the end of the last chapter we left Dick standing on the steps of Mr. Rockwell's residence in Madison Avenue. He had rung the bell and was waiting to have his summons answered. To say that Dick expected to enjoy his visit would not be strictly true. He knew very well that his street education had not qualified him to appear to advantage in fashionable society, and he wished that Fosdick were with him to lend him countenance.

While under the influence of these feelings the door was thrown open, and a servant looked at him inquiringly.

"Is Mr. Rockwell at home?" asked Dick.

"Yes. Would you like to see him?"

"He asked me to call this evening."

"What! Are you the boy that saved Master Johnny from drowning?" asked the servant, her face brightening up, for Johnny was a great favorite in the house.

"I jumped into the water after him," said Dick, modestly.

"I heard Mr. Rockwell say he was expecting you to-night. Come right in. Mistress is very anxious to see you."

Placed a little at his ease by this cordial reception, Dick followed the servant upstairs to a pleasant sitting-room on the second floor. Mr. and Mrs. Rockwell were seated at a centre-table reading the evening papers, while Johnny and his sister Grace were constructing a Tower of Babel with some blocks upon the carpet before the fire.

Dick entered, and stood just within the door, with his cap in his hand, feeling a little embarrassed.

"I am glad to see you, Richard," said Mr. Rockwell, rising from his seat, and advancing to our hero with a pleasant smile. "Mrs. Rockwell has been anxious to see you. My dear, this is the brave boy who saved our little Johnny."

Mrs. Rockwell, a tall, graceful lady, with a smile that quite captivated Dick, offered her hand, and said, earnestly, "My brave boy, I have been wishing to see you. I shudder to think that, but for your prompt courage, I should now be mourning the loss of my dear little Johnny. Accept a mother's thanks for a favor so great that she can never hope to repay it."

Now this acknowledgment was very pleasant to Dick, but it was also very embarrassing. It is difficult to receive praise gracefully. So our hero, not knowing what else to say, stammered out that she was very welcome.

"I understand that you have entered my husband's employment," said Mrs. Rockwell.

"Yes," said Dick. "He was kind enough to take me."

"I hope to make a man of business of our young friend," said Mr. Rockwell. "He will soon feel at home in his new position, and I hope we may find the connection mutually satisfactory."

"Have you a pleasant boarding-place?" asked Mrs. Rockwell.

"Tip-top," said Dick. "I mean pretty good," he added, in a little confusion.

"Where is it?"

"In Bleecker Street," said Dick, very glad that he was not obliged to say Mott Street.

"That is quite a good location," said Mr. Rockwell. "How do you spend your evenings, Richard?"

"In studying with a friend of mine," said Dick. "I want to know something by the time I grow up."

"That is an excellent resolution," said his employer, with warm approval. "I wish more boys of your age were equally sensible. You may depend upon it that a good education is the best preparation for an honorable and useful manhood. What is your friend's name?"

"Henry Fosdick. He rooms with me."

"I am glad you have a friend who shares your tastes. But perhaps you would like to renew your acquaintance with the young gentleman to whom you have rendered so great a service. Johnny has been allowed to stay up beyond his usual bedtime because you were coming. Johnny, come here!"

Johnny rose from his blocks, and came to his mother's side. He was a pleasant-looking little fellow, with a pair of bright eyes, and round, plump cheeks. He looked shyly at Dick.

"Did you ever see this young man?" asked his mother.

"Yes," said Johnny.

"When was it?"

"When I was in the river," said Johnny. "He pulled me out."

"Are you glad to see him?"

"Yes," said Johnny. "What is his name?"

"Dick," said our hero, who somehow could not help feeling, when called Richard, that some other boy was meant.

"Won't you come and help me build a house?" asked little Johnny.

Dick accepted the invitation with pleasure, feeling more at home with children than with older persons.

"This is sister Grace," said Johnny, with an offhand introduction.

"I saw you on the boat," said Dick.

"Yes," said Grace, "I was there. Oh, how frightened I was when Johnny fell into the water! I don't see how you dared to jump in after him."

"Oh, I've been in swimming many a time. I don't mind it," said Dick.

"I s'pose you're used to it, like the fishes," said Johnny. "I'm glad I'm not a fish. I shouldn't like to live in the water."

"I don't think I should, either," said Dick. "Now, what do you think the fishes do when it rains?"

"I do not know."

"They go down to the bottom of the sea to get out of the wet."

"Isn't it wet down at the bottom of the sea?" asked Johnny, in good faith.

"Of course it is, you little goose," said Grace, with an air of superior wisdom.

"Will you make me a house?" said Johnny.

"What kind of a house do you want?" said Dick, seating himself on the carpet, and taking up the blocks.

"Any kind," said Johnny.

Dick, beginning to feel quite at home with the children, erected an imposing-looking house, leaving little spaces for the doors and windows.

"That's better than the house Grace made," said Johnny, looking at it with complacency.

"But it won't last very long," said Dick. "You'd better sell it before it tumbles over."

"Do you own any houses?" asked Johnny.

"Not many," said Dick, smiling.

"My father owns this house," said Johnny, positively. "He paid fifty dollars for it."

"I didn't think houses were so cheap," said Dick. "I'd like to buy one at that price."

"You're a little goose, Johnny," said Grace. "He gave as much as five hundred dollars."

"Grace doesn't know much more about the price of real estate than Johnny," said Mr. Rockwell.

"Didn't the house cost as much as five hundred dollars?" asked Grace.

"As much as that certainly, my dear."

Just then, by an unguarded movement of Johnny's foot, the edifice of blocks reared by Dick became a confused ruin.

"I've got tired of building houses," he announced, "Won't you tell me a story, Dick?"

"I don't think I know any," said our hero.

"Here is a book of pictures," said his mother, bringing one from the table. "Perhaps your new friend will show them to you."

Dick took the book, and felt very glad that he had learned to read. Otherwise he might have been considerably embarrassed.

The children asked a great many questions of Dick about the pictures, some of which he could not answer. Johnny, on being shown the picture of a Turkish mosque, asked if that was the place where the turkeys went to church.

"If there was any place for a goose to go to church, you'd go there," said his sister.

"I aint a goose any more than you are," said Johnny, indignantly; "am I, Dick?"

Just then the servant came in to carry the children to bed, and, considerably against their wishes, they were obliged to withdraw.

"Come again, Dick," said Johnny.

"Thank you," said Dick. "Good-night."

"Good-night," said the two children, and the door closed upon them.

"I think I'll be going," said Dick, who did not feel quite so much at ease, now that his young friends had left him.

"Wait a few minutes," said Mrs. Rockwell.

She rang the bell, and a servant brought up some cake and apples, of which Dick was invited to partake.

I need not detail the conversation; but Mrs. Rockwell, with the tact of a genuine lady, managed to draw out Dick, and put him quite at his ease.

"How old are you, Richard?" she asked.

"Fifteen," said Dick; "goin' on sixteen."

"You are getting to be quite a young man,—old enough to wear a watch. Have you one?"

"No," said Dick, not suspecting the motive that led to her question.

"Will you allow me the pleasure of supplying the deficiency?" said Mrs. Rockwell.

As she spoke, she drew from a box at her side a very neat gold watch and chain, and placed it in Dick's hands.

Our hero was so astonished at first that he could scarcely believe that this valuable present was intended for him.

"Is it for me?" he asked, hesitatingly.

"Yes," said Mrs. Rockwell, smiling pleasantly. "I hope you will find it of service."

"It is too much," said Dick. "I do not deserve it."

"You must let me be the judge of that," said the lady, kindly. "Here is the key; I nearly forgot to give it to you. I suppose you know how to wind it up?"

"Yes," said Dick. "I understand that. I am *very* much obliged to you."

"You are very welcome. Whenever you look at it, let it remind you that under all circumstances you can rely upon the friendship of Johnny's parents."

Dick slipped the watch into a watch-pocket in his vest, for which he had never before had any use, and attached the chain to his button-hole.

"How beautiful it is!" he said, in tones of admiration.

"It was bought at Ball & Black's," said Mrs. Rockwell. "If it should not keep good time, or anything should happen to it, I advise you to take it there, and they will repair it for you."

Dick perceived by his new watch that it was nearly ten o'clock, and rose to go. He was kindly invited to renew his visit, and promised to do so. Just as he was leaving the room, Mr. Rockwell handed a sealed envelope to Dick, saying, "Put this in your pocket, Richard. It will be time enough to open it when you get home."

Dick sped home much more quickly than he had come. He thought with delight of Fosdick's surprise when he should see the new watch and chain, and also with pardonable exultation of the sensation he would produce at the table when he carelessly drew out his watch to see what time it was.

When he reached his boarding-house, and went upstairs, he found Fosdick sitting up for him.

"Well, Dick, what sort of a time did you have?" he asked.

"Tip-top," said Dick.

"Who did you see?"

"Mr. and Mrs. Rockwell, and two children,—Johnny, the one I fished out of the water, and his sister, Grace. Johnny's a jolly little chap, and his sister is a nice girl."

"Halloa, what's that?" asked Fosdick, suddenly espying the watch-chain.

"What do you think of my new watch?" asked Dick, drawing it out.

"Do you mean to say it is yours?"

"Yes. Mrs. Rockwell gave it to me."

"It's a regular beauty. Mr. Henderson has got one that he paid a hundred dollars for; but it isn't as nice as yours."

"Seems to me I have no end of luck," said Dick. "I'll be a young man of fortun' before I know it."

"People will think you are now, when they see you wear such a watch as that."

"Johnny Nolan'd think I stole it, if he should see it," said Dick. "Poor chap! I wish some luck would come to him. I saw him to-day lookin' just as I used to before I met Frank."

"There's some difference between then and now, Dick."

"Yes. I was a rough chap in them days."

"In those days, Dick."

"In those days, and I don't know but I am now, but I'm trying to improve. With you to help me, I think I'll grow up respectable."

"I hope we both will, Dick. But who's that letter from that you've just taken out of your pocket?"

"Oh, I forgot. Mr. Rockwell handed it to me just before I came away, and told me not to open it till I got home. P'r'aps it says that he hasn't no more occasion for my valuable services."

"That isn't very likely, considering the present you have brought home. But open it; I am curious to see what is in it."

The envelope was cut open, and a piece of paper dropped out.

Fosdick picked it up, and to his inexpressible amazement ascertained that it was a check on the Park Bank for the sum of one thousand dollars made payable to Richard Hunter, or order.

"A thousand dollars!" repeated Dick, overwhelmed with astonishment; "you're only foolin' me. P'r'aps it's ten dollars."

"No, it's a thousand dollars. Read it yourself if you don't believe it."

"I wish you'd pinch me, Fosdick," said Dick, seriously.

"Certainly, if you wish it."

"That's enough," said Dick, hastily. "I only wanted to make sure I wasn't dreamin'. I can't believe I'm worth a thousand dollars."

"You're a lucky fellow, Dick," said Fosdick, "and you deserve your luck. I'm heartily glad of it."

"About the best luck I ever had was in meeting you," said Dick, affectionately. "I'm goin' to give you half the money."

"No, you're not, Dick. Thank you all the same," said Fosdick, decidedly. "It was meant for you, and you must keep it. I'll get along well enough. If I don't, I know you'll help me."

"But I wish you'd take half the money."

"No, Dick, it wouldn't be right. But your new watch says it's getting late, and we had better go to bed."

It was some time before Dick fell asleep. His good luck had so excited him that he found it difficult to calm down sufficiently to sink into a quiet slumber.

CHAPTER VI.

MR. GILBERT IS ASTONISHED.

When Dick woke up in the morning the first thing he thought of was his watch, the next the check which he had received from Mr. Rockwell.

"I'll go to the bank this morning, and get my money," said he.

"How are you going to invest it, Dick?" asked Fosdick.

"I don't know," said Dick. "I'll put it in the savings bank till I decide. That'll make more'n eleven hundred dollars. I didn't use to think I ever'd be worth that, when I slept in boxes and old wagons."

"Eleven hundred dollars at six per cent. interest will yield you sixty-six dollars a year."

"So it will," said Dick, "and all without working. I tell you what, Fosdick, at this rate I'll soon be a man of fortune."

"Yes, if you can make a thousand dollars a day."

"I wonder what old Gilbert'll say when he sees it," said Dick.

"Who's he?"

"He's the book-keeper. He aint very fond of me."

"What has he against you?"

"He thinks I don't treat him with proper respect," said Dick. "Besides he tried to get his cousin Roswell Crawford in, but he couldn't."

"Then it seems both of us have interfered with Roswell."

"He's got a place now. I guess he's the senior partner by the way he talks."

The breakfast-bell rang, and the boys went down to breakfast. Clifton was down already, and was standing in front of stove. Being an observing young man he at once noticed Dick's watch-chain.

"Halloa, Hunter!" said he; "I didn't know you had a watch."

"I didn't know it myself till last night," said Dick.

"Where did you get it?"

"It came from Ball & Black's," said our hero, willing to mystify him.

"That's a nice chain,—solid gold, eh?"

"Do you think I'd wear anything else?" asked Dick, loftily.

"Will you allow me to look at the watch?"

"Certainly," said Dick, drawing it from his pocket, and submitting it to Clifton's inspection.

"It's a regular beauty," said the young man, enthusiastically. "Do you mind telling how much you paid for it?"

"How much do you think?"

"A hundred dollars?"

"It cost all of that," said Dick, confidently. "If you see one for sale at that price, just let me know, and I'll buy it for a speculation."

"You must be getting a pretty good salary to buy such a watch as that."

"Pretty good," said Dick, carelessly.

Mr. Clifton was rather a shallow young man, who was fond of show, and had a great respect for those who were able to make it. When Dick first came to the boarding-house he looked down upon him as a boy; but now that he proved to be the possessor of an elegant gold watch and chain, and might, therefore, be regarded

25

as in prosperous circumstances, he conceived a high respect for him. The truth was that Clifton himself only got two dollars a week more than Dick, yet he paid eight dollars a week for board, and spent the rest in dress. His reputation among tailors was not the best, being always more ready to order new clothes than to pay for them.

While they were talking the rest of the boarders entered, and breakfast commenced. Miss Peyton was there, of course.

"How did you find your friends in Madison Avenue last evening, Mr. Hunter?" she inquired.

"They were all up and dressed," said Dick. "They sent their partic'lar regards to you."

"Oh, you wicked story-teller!" simpered Miss Peyton; "just as if I'd believe such nonsense. Have they got a nice house?"

"Beautiful," said Dick. "I haven't seen any like it since I called on Queen Victoria last year."

"How is the house furnished?"

"Well," said Dick, "as near as I can remember, there's diamonds worked in the carpet, and all the tables and chairs is of gold. They'd be rather hard to set on if it twan't for the velvet cushions."

"Aint you afraid to tell such stories, Mr. Hunter? Mr. Fosdick, you will have to talk to your friend."

"I am afraid it wouldn't do much good, Miss Peyton, if you fail to cure him."

"Mr. Hunter has just been investing in a handsome watch," remarked Clifton, passing his cup for a second cup of coffee.

"Oh, do let me look at it! I dote on watches," said Miss Peyton.

"Certainly," said Dick; and he detached the chain from his button-hole, and passed the watch across the table.

"It's a perfect little love," said Miss Peyton, enthusiastically. "Isn't it, Mrs. Browning?"

"It is very beautiful, certainly," said the landlady. She could not help feeling surprised that Dick, who, it will be remembered, had represented himself at his first visit to be in limited circumstances, and now occupied one of her cheapest rooms, could afford to purchase an article which was evidently so costly.

"Where did you buy it, Mr. Hunter?" asked another boarder.

"I did not buy it at all," said Dick, deciding to let it be known how it came into his possession. "It was given to me."

"Perhaps you'll mention my name to the person that gave it to you," said Mr. Clifton. "If he's got any more to dispose of in that way, I should like to come in for one."

"How do you know but it may have come from a *lady* friend, Mr. Clifton?" said Miss Peyton, slyly.

"How is that, Hunter?"

"I haven't had any presents from any of my lady friends yet," said Dick. "Perhaps I may some time."

"You don't mean anybody in particular, of course, Mr. Hunter?" said Miss Peyton.

"Oh, no, of course not."

This conversation may seem scarcely worth recording, but it will serve to illustrate the character of Dick's fellow-boarders. Miss Peyton was rather silly and affected, but she was good-natured, and Dick felt more at home with her than he would have done had she been a lady like Mrs. Rockwell, for instance. It got to be the custom with Dick and Fosdick to remain in the parlor a short time after supper, or rather dinner, for this was the third meal, and Fosdick joined the young lady in singing. Dick unfortunately had not been gifted by nature with a voice attuned to melody, and he participated only as a listener, in which capacity he enjoyed the entertainment.

After breakfast Dick set out for the store as usual. He felt unusually happy and independent as he walked along. The check in his pocket made him feel rich. He wondered how it would be best to invest his money so as to yield him the largest return. He wisely decided to take Mr. Murdock, the head clerk, into his confidence, and ask his advice upon this point.

When Dick arrived at the store neither Mr. Gilbert nor Mr. Murdock had yet arrived. Half an hour later the latter came, and five minutes after him the book-keeper.

The latter noticed that the morning paper appeared to have been disturbed, and, glad of any opportunity to find fault with Dick, said, angrily, "So you've been reading the paper instead of minding your work, have you? I'll report you to Mr. Rockwell."

"Thank you," said Dick, "you're very kind. Are you sure I read the paper? Is there any news missin' out of it?"

"You're an impudent boy," said the book-keeper, provoked. He wanted to overawe Dick; but somehow Dick wouldn't be overawed. Evidently he did not entertain as much respect for the book-keeper as that gentleman felt to be his due. That a mere errand-boy should bandy words with a gentleman in his position seemed to Mr. Gilbert highly reprehensible.

"You're an impudent boy!" repeated Gilbert, sharply, finding Dick did not reply to his first charge.

"I heard you make that remark before," said Dick, quietly.

Now there was nothing out of the way in Dick's tone, which was perfectly respectful, and he only stated a fact; but the book-keeper became still more angry.

"Who rumpled that paper?" he asked.

"Suppose you ask Mr. Murdock?" said Dick.

"Did he come in here?" asked Gilbert, cooling down, for it was against Dick that his charge was made, and not against the head clerk. As to the paper, he really cared nothing.

"Yes," said Dick.

"Then it's all right. I supposed you had been idling your time over the paper. Go and ask Mr. Murdock what time it is. I left my watch at home."

"It's half past eight," said Dick, drawing out his watch.

Up to this time the book-keeper had not noticed Dick's watch-chain. Now that his attention was drawn not only to that, but to the beautiful gold watch which Dick carried, he was not a little surprised.

"Whose watch is that?" he asked, abruptly.

"Mine," said Dick, briefly, rather enjoying the book-keeper's surprise.

"How did you come by it?"

"Honestly," said Dick.

"Is it gold, or only plated?"

"It's gold."

"Humph! Did you buy it, or was it given you?"

"Well," said Dick, "I didn't buy it."

"Did you say it was yours?"

"Yes."

Gilbert looked at Dick in surprise. Our hero was becoming more and more an enigma to him. That a boy in Dick's position should have a gold watch given him, especially now that he had learned from his cousin Roswell the nature of Dick's former employment, seemed indeed wonderful.

"Let me look at your watch a minute," he said.

Dick handed it to him.

"It seems to be a very good one," he said.

"Yes," said Dick; "I aint proud. It's as good as I want to wear."

"It looks entirely out of place on such a boy as you," said the book-keeper, sharply.

"Perhaps it would look better on you," suggested our hero, innocently.

"Yes, it would be more appropriate for me to wear than you. You're not old enough to be trusted with a watch; least of all with such a good one as that."

"Perhaps you'd be kind enough to mention it to the one that gave it to me."

"Whoever gave it to you didn't show much judgment," said Gilbert, in the same pleasant way. "Who was it?"

"It was Mrs. Rockwell."

If a bombshell had exploded in the office, it could hardly have taken Gilbert more by surprise.

"Who did you say?" he repeated, thinking his ears might have deceived him.

"Mrs. Rockwell," said Dick, once more.

The book-keeper could hardly suppress a low whistle.

"When did she give it to you?"

"Last evening."

"Were you up there?"

"Yes."

"Did Mr. Rockwell invite you?"

"Yes."

Just then Dick was called away by Mr. Murdock, who had some work for him to do.

"There's something mighty queer in all this," thought the book-keeper. "What Mr. Rockwell can see in that boy, I don't understand. He's an impudent young rascal, and I'll get him turned off if it's a possible thing."

CHAPTER VII.

A FINANCIAL DISCUSSION.

In the course of the morning Dick called at the Park Bank, and presented the check which was made payable to himself. His employer had accompanied him to the bank on a previous day, and introduced him to the cashier as one who was authorized to receive and pay over money for the firm. Dick therefore found no difficulty in obtaining his money, though the fact that the check was made payable to him created some surprise.

"Your salary seems to be a large one," said the teller, as he handed our hero ten bills of a hundred dollars each.

"Yes," said Dick, "my services are very valooable."

On leaving the bank, Dick went to the savings bank, and presented his book.

"How much do you wish to deposit?"

"A thousand dollars," said Dick, briefly.

The bank officer looked at him in surprise.

"How much did you say?" he repeated.

"A thousand dollars."

"No nonsense, young man! My time is too valuable," said the other, impatiently.

He was justified in his incredulity, since Dick's deposits hitherto had been in sums of from one to five dollars.

"If you don't want to take the money, I can go somewhere else," said our hero, who was now on his dignity. "I have a thousand dollars to deposit. Here it is."

The bank officer took the money, and counted it over in considerable surprise.

"Business is improving,—isn't it?" he said.

"Yes," said Dick. "I made all that money in one day."

"If you should want a partner, call round and see me."

"All right. I won't forget."

Dick took the bank-book, and, putting it in his inside coat-pocket, buttoned up his coat, and hurried back to the store. His reflections were of a very agreeable nature, as he thought of his large deposit in the savings bank, and he could not help feeling that he had been born under a lucky star.

Nothing of consequence transpired in the store that day. Dick was attentive to his duties. He was determined to learn the business as rapidly as possible, not only because he felt grateful to Mr. Rockwell for his kindness, but also because he knew that this was the best thing for his future prospects. Mr. Murdock, who has already been mentioned, was of service to him in this respect. He was himself an excellent business man, and very conscientious in the discharge of his duties. He required the same fidelity of others. He had observed Dick closely, and was attracted towards him by his evident desire to give satisfaction, as well as by his frank, open face. He resolved to help him along, more especially when he saw the manner in which he was treated by the book-keeper. To tell the truth, Mr. Gilbert was not a favorite with Mr. Murdock. He understood his business, to be sure, and, so far as Mr. Murdock knew, kept the books correctly. But personally he was not agreeable, and the head salesman doubted whether his integrity was what it should have been. So, altogether, he made up his mind to help Dick on as well as he could, and take pains to instruct him in the business.

Dick, on his side, was pleased with Mr. Murdock, and determined to make him a confidant in the matter of his sudden accession of fortune.

He took an opportunity, therefore, during the day, to say to him, "Mr. Murdock, I want to ask your advice about something."

"Well, my lad, what is it?" said his friend, kindly. "If it's about choosing a wife, I don't know whether my advice will be good for much."

"It isn't that," said Dick. "Next year'll be soon enough for that."

"So I should think. Well, if it's nothing of that sort, what is it?"

"It's about investing some money. I thought you might be able to advise me."

"How much is it?" asked Mr. Murdock, supposing the sum could not be more than fifty or sixty dollars.

"Eleven hundred dollars," said Dick.

"How much?" demanded the salesman, in surprise.

"Eleven hundred dollars."

"Is it your own?"

"Yes."

"Of course you couldn't have earned so much. Was it left to you?"

"I'll tell you all about it," said Dick. "I wouldn't tell Mr. Gilbert, and I don't mean he shall know it, but I'd just as lieves tell you. Do you know why Mr. Rockwell gave me this place?"

"No; I've wondered a little, not at that, but at his giving you so much higher pay than boys usually receive."

"Then I'll tell you."

Dick proceeded to give an account of the manner in which he had rescued little Johnny from drowning, as related in the adventures of "Ragged Dick."

"It was a brave act," said Mr. Murdock.

"It was nothing at all," said Dick, modestly. "I could swim like a duck, and I didn't mind the wetting."

"But you ran the risk of drowning."

"I didn't think of that."

"If you had been a coward or a selfish boy, it would have been the first thing you would have thought of. So Mr. Rockwell gave you this place in acknowledgment of your service. I am glad he did. You deserve it."

"He has done more," said Dick. Then he related the events of the evening previous, and told Mr. Murdock of the two gifts he had received. "So, with the money I had before, I have now eleven hundred dollars," Dick concluded. "Shall I leave it in the savings bank, or can I do better with it?"

"I'll tell you what I think will be a good investment," said Mr. Murdock. "I know a party who owns four adjoining lots on Forty-Fifth Street. He is pressed for money, and wishes to dispose of them. He offered them to me at twenty-two hundred dollars, half cash. I offered him a thousand dollars cash for two of them, but he wishes to sell the whole together. I think it will be an excellent speculation, for the laying out of Central Park is carrying up the price of lots in the neighborhood rapidly."

"Why didn't you buy them, then?"

"Because I didn't want to buy anything that I couldn't pay for at once. I've got a wife and three children to look out for, and so I can save money but slowly. If I only had myself to take care of, I wouldn't hesitate."

"Can't we club together, and buy it?" suggested Dick, eagerly.

"That is just what I was going to propose. I think the owner will take two thousand dollars down for the lots. That will be a thousand dollars apiece. I've got that money, and so have you. What do you think of it?"

"Tip-top," said Dick, enthusiastically. "It's just what I'd like to do."

"Of course it wouldn't bring us in anything, but would, instead, be an expense for the present, as we should have to pay taxes on it. On the other hand, you could invest the money in bank-stock, so as to receive seventy or eighty dollars annually at interest. You must decide which investment you prefer. The land we may have to keep on hand four or five years, paying taxes yearly."

"But the price'll go up."

"There is no doubt of that. The city is extending northwards rapidly. I shouldn't be surprised if the lots would bring a thousand dollars apiece in less than five years. This would be equal to a very handsome interest."

"I'm in for buying 'em," said Dick. "So, if you'll see the owner, I'll have the money all ready whenever you want it."

"Very well, but perhaps you would like to see them first. We'll manage to get off an hour earlier than usual this afternoon, and go up and take a look at them."

"It seems to me Mr. Murdock and that boy are pretty thick together," said the book-keeper, glancing through the glass partition. He could see that they were conversing earnestly, but of course couldn't hear a word that was said. "What he or Mr. Rockwell can see in the young rascal passes my comprehension."

He called sharply to Dick, and ordered him to go to the post-office for letters.

"All right," said Dick.

"And mind you don't loiter by the way," said the book-keeper, sharply. "You were gone long enough at the bank this morning. Did you come right back?"

"No," said Dick.

"Why didn't you?"

"There was somewhere else I wanted to go."

31

"On your own business, or Mr. Rockwell's?"

"On my own business."

"So I thought. I shall report you to Mr. Rockwell," said Gilbert, triumphantly.

"I wouldn't, if I were you," said Dick, coolly.

"And why not, you young rascal?"

"Because he knows it already."

"Knows it already," repeated the book-keeper, discomfited. "Well, I hope he gave you a good scolding."

"I am sorry to disappoint you," said Dick; "but he knows it, because he gave me leave to go."

"I don't believe it," said Gilbert, mortified to find that Dick was in the right after all.

"Then perhaps you'd better ask Mr. Rockwell."

"I will," said Gilbert, who really had no intention of doing so. "You must have had some very urgent private business," he added, with a sneer.

"You're right, there," said Dick.

"Playing marbles with some of your ragamuffin friends, I suppose."

"Playin' marbles is a very refined and intellectual amusement," said Dick; "but I don't play marbles in business hours."

"Where did you go?" said the book-keeper, impatiently. "I don't want any of your impertinence."

"I went to the savings bank," said Dick.

"I suppose you have a very large account there," sneered Gilbert.

"Yes," said Dick, quietly; "pretty large."

"It's to be hoped you won't withdraw your patronage, or the bank might fail."

"Then I won't," said Dick. "Shall I go to the post-office now?"

"Yes, and be quick about it."

The book-keeper had some curiosity as to the amount of Dick's account at the savings bank, but there was no good chance for him to inquire, and he accordingly returned to his writing, more prejudiced against Dick than ever.

On the whole, I have some doubts whether Dick's manner was quite as respectful as it ought to have been to one who was older and higher in office than himself. I should not recommend my young readers to imitate him in this respect. But it is my business to describe Dick just as he was, and I have already said that he was not a model boy. Still in most respects he tried to do what was right, and it must be admitted that the book-keeper's treatment of him was not likely to inspire much attachment or respect. Dick had no difficulty in perceiving the dislike entertained by Gilbert for him, and he was beginning to cherish a similar feeling towards the book-keeper. He determined, however, to give him no cause of complaint, so far as he was entitled to command his services; but it must be confessed he found much more satisfaction in obeying Mr. Rockwell and Mr. Murdock.

CHAPTER VIII.

NEW PLANS.

At the close of the afternoon, as had been proposed, Mr. Murdock, accompanied by Dick, rode up as far as Forty-Fifth Street, to look at the lots which he had suggested buying. They were located in a very eligible situation, between Fifth and Sixth Avenues. Some of my young readers may not be aware that the dimensions of a city lot are twenty-five feet front by one hundred feet in depth. The four lots together made a plot of one hundred feet by one hundred, or a little less than quarter of an acre. In the country the whole would scarcely have been considered sufficient for a house with a good yard in front; but if people choose to live in the city they must make up their minds to be crowded.

"It looks small,—don't it?" said Dick. "I shouldn't think there was four lots there."

"Yes," said Mr. Murdock, "they are of the regular size. Some lots are only twenty feet wide. These are twenty-five. They don't look so large before they are built on."

"Well," said Dick, "I'm in for buying them."

"I think it will be a good investment for both of us," said Mr. Murdock.

"The money shall be ready whenever you want it," said Dick.

"Very well. I will see the owner to-morrow, or rather this evening, as it is best to be prompt, lest we might lose so favorable a bargain. I will make the best terms I can with him, and let you know the result to-morrow."

"All right!" said Dick. "Good-night, Mr. Murdock."

"Good-night. By-the-by, why won't you come round and take supper with us? My wife and children will be glad to make your acquaintance."

"Thank you," said Dick. "I will come some other evening with pleasure; but if I stay away without saying anything about it, Fosdick won't know what's become of me."

Dick got back to Bleecker Street a little late for dinner. When he entered the dining-room, the remainder of the boarders were seated at the table.

"Come, Mr. Hunter, you must render an account of yourself," said Miss Peyton, playfully. "Why are you late this evening?"

"Suppose I don't tell," said Dick.

"Then you must pay a fine,—mustn't he, Mrs. Browning?"

"That depends upon who is to benefit by the fines," said the landlady. "If they are to be paid to me, I shall be decidedly in favor of it. That reminds me that you were late to breakfast this morning, Miss Peyton."

"Oh, ladies mustn't be expected to pay fines," said Miss Peyton, shaking her ringlets. "They never have any money, you know."

"Then I think we must let Mr. Hunter off," said Mrs. Browning.

"If he will tell us what has detained him. You must excuse my curiosity, Mr. Hunter, but ladies, you know, are privileged to be curious."

"I don't mind telling," said Dick, helping himself to a piece of toast. "I'm talking of buying some lots up-town, and went up with a friend to look at them."

Fosdick looked at Dick, inquiringly, not knowing if he were in earnest or not.

"Indeed!" said Mr. Clifton. "May I inquire where the lots are situated?"

"I'll tell you if I buy them," said Dick; "but I don't want to run the risk of losing them."

"You needn't be afraid of my cutting you out," said Clifton. "I paid my washerwoman this morning, and haven't got but a dollar and a half over. I suppose that won't buy the property."

"I wish it would," said Dick. "In that case I'd buy half a dozen lots."

"I suppose, from your investing in lots, Mr. Hunter, that you are thinking of getting married, and living in a house of your own," said Miss Peyton, simpering.

"No," said Dick, "I shan't get married for a year. Nobody ought to be married before they're seventeen."

"That's just my age," said Miss Peyton.

Mr. Clifton afterwards informed Dick that Miss Peyton was twenty-five, but did not mention how he had ascertained. He likewise added that when he first came to the boarding-house, she had tried her fascinations upon him.

"She'd have married me in a minute," he said complacently; "but I'm too old a bird to be caught that way. When you see Mrs. Clifton, gentlemen, you'll see style and beauty, and—*money*," he added, after a moment's reflection.

Mr. Clifton had a tolerably good opinion of himself, as may be inferred from this remark. In fact, he valued himself rather more highly than the ladies appeared to do; but such cases are not remarkable.

"Mrs. Clifton will be a lucky woman," said Dick, with a sober face.

"You're very kind to say so," said Mr. Clifton, modestly. "I believe I'm tolerably good-looking, and nobody'll deny that I've got style. But money,—that's my weak point. You couldn't lend me five dollars, could you, till next week?"

"I'm afraid not," said Dick. "My up-town lots cost so much, and then there'll be the taxes afterwards."

"Oh, it's of no consequence. I thought a little of going to the opera to-night, and I need a new pair of gloves. It costs a sight to keep a fellow in gloves."

"So it does," said Dick. "I bought a pair for fifty cents six months ago, and now I've got to buy another pair."

"Ha, ha! good joke! By the way, I wonder you fellows don't take a better room."

"Why should we? Isn't this good enough?" asked Fosdick.

"Oh, it's comfortable and all that," said Clifton; "but you know what I mean. You wouldn't want any of your fashionable friends to call upon you here."

"That's a fact," said Dick. "Suppose," he said, turning to Fosdick, with a twinkle in his eye, "Johnny Nolan should call upon us here. What would he think of our living in such a room?"

"He would probably be surprised," said Fosdick, entering into the joke.

"Is he one of your Madison-Avenue friends?" asked Clifton, a little mystified.

"I don't know where he lives," said Dick, with truth; "but he's a friend of mine, in business down town."

"Wholesale or retail?"

"Retail I should say,—shouldn't you, Fosdick?"

"Yes," said Fosdick, amused at Clifton's evident mystification.

"Well, good-evening, gents," said Clifton, sauntering out of the room. "Call and see me when you haven't anything better to do."

"Thank you. Good-night."

"Were you in earnest, Dick, about the up-town lots," asked Fosdick, after Clifton had left the room.

"Yes," said Dick. "It's an investment that Mr. Murdock advised. I'll tell you about it, and then you can tell me what you think of it."

Dick thereupon gave an account of the conversation that had taken place between him and the head clerk, and what they proposed to do. "What do you think of it?" he concluded.

"I have no doubt it is an excellent plan," said Fosdick; "but of course my opinion isn't worth much. I don't see but you stand a chance to be a rich man some time, Dick."

"By the time I get to be a hundred," said Dick.

"A good while before that, I presume. But there's something else we must not forget."

"What is that?"

"Money is a good thing to have, but a good education is better. I was thinking to-day that since we have come here we haven't done any studying to amount to anything."

"That is true."

"And the sooner we begin the better."

"All right. I agree to that."

"But we shall need assistance. I've taught you about all I know myself, and now we want to go higher."

"What shall we do?"

"I'll tell you, Dick. Have you noticed the young man that has a room just opposite ours?"

"His name is Layton,—isn't it?"

"Yes."

"What about him?"

"I heard yesterday that he was a teacher in a private school. We might engage him to teach us in the evening, or, at any rate, see if he is willing."

"All right. Is he in now, I wonder?"

"Yes. I heard him go into his room a few minutes since."

"Very well; suppose we go in and speak to him."

The boys at once acted upon this suggestion, and, crossing the entry, knocked at the door.

"Come in!" said a voice from within.

The door being opened, they found themselves in the presence of a young man of pleasant appearance, apparently about twenty-five years of age.

"Good-evening, gentlemen," he said. "I am glad to see you. Will you have seats?"

"Thank you," said Fosdick. "We came in on a little business. I understand you are a teacher, Mr. Layton."

"Yes, I am engaged in a private school in the city."

"My friend and myself are engaged in business during the day, but we feel that our education is quite deficient, and we want to make arrangements to study evenings. We cannot do this to advantage without assistance. Are you occupied during the evenings?"

"No, I am not."

"Perhaps you would not like teaching in the evening, after being engaged in the daytime."

"On the contrary, I have been hoping to secure scholars; but I hardly knew how to set about it."

"Are you acquainted with the French language, Mr. Layton?"

"Yes, I am tolerably familiar with it. I studied it at college with a native teacher."

"If you are a college graduate, then, you will be able to teach us whatever we desire to learn. But I am afraid we may not be able to make it worth your while. We have neither of us large salaries. But if four dollars a week—two dollars for each of us—would be satisfactory—"

"I shall be satisfied with it," said Mr. Layton. "In fact," he added, frankly, "I shall consider it quite a welcome addition to my salary. My father died a year since, and my mother and sister are compelled to depend upon me in part for support. But I have not been able to do as much for them as I wished. This addition to my earnings will give me the means of increasing their comforts."

"Then it will be a pleasant arrangement all round," said Fosdick. "What would you advise us to study?"

After a few inquiries as to their present attainments, Mr. Layton recommended a course of mathematics, beginning with algebra, history, and the French language. He gave the boys a list of the books they would be likely to need.

The next evening the boys commenced studying, and determined to devote an hour and a half each evening to mental improvement. They found Mr. Layton an excellent teacher, and he on his side found them very apt pupils.

Dick had an active, intelligent mind, and an excellent capacity, and Fosdick had always had a thirst for learning, which he was now able to gratify. As his salary would have been insufficient to pay his expenses and the teacher besides, he was obliged to have recourse to his little fund in the savings bank. Dick offered to assist him, but Fosdick would not consent. Just as his savings were about exhausted, his wages were raised two dollars a week, and this enabled him to continue the arrangement without assistance.

In the course of a few weeks the boys commenced reading French, and found it quite interesting.

CHAPTER IX.

ROSWELL CRAWFORD AT HOME.

While Fosdick and Dick are devoting their evenings to study, under the guidance of Mr. Layton, we will direct the reader's attention to a young gentleman who considered himself infinitely superior in the social scale to either. Roswell Crawford could never forget that Dick had once been a boot-black, and looked upon it as an outrage that such a boy should be earning a salary of ten dollars a week, while he—a gentleman's son—was only paid four, which he regarded as a beggarly pittance. Roswell's father had once kept a small dry goods store on Broadway, but failed after being in business a little less than a year. This constituted his claim to gentility. After his failure, Mr. Crawford tried several kinds of business, without succeeding in any. His habits were not strictly temperate, and he had died two years previous. His wife hired a house in Clinton Place, and took boarders, barely succeeding in making both ends meet at the end of the year. The truth was that she was not a good manager, and preferred to talk of her gentility and former wealth to looking after the affairs of the household. She was very much like her son in this respect.

Among Mrs. Crawford's boarders was Mr. Gilbert, who is already known to the reader as the book-keeper of Rockwell & Cooper. It has been mentioned also that he was Roswell's cousin, being a son of Mrs. Crawford's only brother. He, too, was not unlike his aunt and cousin, and all three combined to hate and despise Dick, whom Mrs. Crawford saw fit to regard as her son's successful rival.

"How's the boot-black, Cousin James?" asked Roswell, on the evening succeeding that which Dick had passed at Mr. Rockwell's.

"Putting on airs worse than ever," replied Gilbert.

"Mr. Rockwell has a singular taste, to say the least," said Mrs. Crawford, "or he wouldn't hire a boy from the streets, and give him such extravagant wages. To pay such a vagabond ten dollars a week, when a boy of good family, like Roswell, can get but four, is perfectly ridiculous."

"I don't believe he gets so much," said Roswell. "It's only one of his big stories."

"You're mistaken there," said Gilbert. "He does get exactly that."

"Are you sure of it?"

"I ought to be, since I received directions from Mr. Rockwell to-day to pay him that amount to-morrow night, that being the end of the week."

"I never heard of such a thing!" ejaculated Mrs. Crawford. "The man must be a simpleton."

"If he is, there's another besides him."

"Who do you mean?"

"Mrs. Rockwell."

"Has she made acquaintance with the boot-black, then?" asked Roswell, with a sneer.

"Yes, he visited them last evening at their house."

"Did he tell you so?"

"Yes."

"I should think they'd feel honored by such a visitor."

"Probably they did, for Mrs. Rockwell made him a present of a gold watch."

"What!" exclaimed Roswell and his mother in concert.

"It's true. I sent him out to ask the time to-day, when he pulled out a new gold watch with an air of importance, and told me the time."

"Was it a good watch?"

"A very handsome one. It must have cost, with the chain, a hundred and twenty-five dollars."

"The idea of a boot-black with a gold watch!" exclaimed Roswell, with a sneer. "It's about as appropriate as a pig in a silk dress."

"I can't understand it at all," said Mrs. Crawford. "It can't be that he's a poor relation of theirs, can it?"

"I should say not. Mr. Rockwell wouldn't be likely to have a relation reduced to blacking boots."

"Is the boy so attractive, then? What does he look like?"

"He's as bold as brass, and hasn't got any manners nor education," said Roswell.

Poor Dick! His ears ought to have tingled, considering the complimentary things that were said of him this evening. But luckily he knew nothing about it, and, if he had, it is doubtful whether it would have troubled him much. He was independent in his ideas, and didn't trouble himself much about the opinion of others, as long as he felt that he was doing right as nearly as he knew how.

"Do you think this strange fancy of Mr. Rockwell's is going to last?" inquired Mrs. Crawford. "I wish Roswell could have got in there."

"So do I, but I couldn't accomplish it."

"If this boy should fall out of favor, there might be a chance for Roswell yet; don't you think so?" asked Mrs. Crawford.

"I wish there might," said Roswell. "I'd like to see that beggar's pride humbled. Besides, four dollars a week is such a miserable salary."

"You thought yourself lucky when you got it."

"So I did; but that was before I found out how much this boot-black was getting."

"Well," said Gilbert, "he isn't a favorite of mine, as you know well enough. If there's anything I can do to oust him, I shall do it."

"Couldn't you leave some money in his way? He might be tempted to steal it."

"I don't know yet what course would be best. I'll try to get him into trouble of some kind. But I can tell better by and by what to do."

Gilbert went up to his room, and Mrs. Crawford and Roswell were left alone.

"I wish you were at Rockwell & Cooper's, Roswell," said his mother.

"So do I, mother; but it's no use wishing."

"I don't know about that. Your cousin ought to have some influence there."

"The boot-black's in the way."

"He may not be in the way always. Your cousin may detect him in something that will cause his discharge."

"Even if he does, I've tried once to get in there, and didn't succeed. They didn't seem to take a fancy to me."

"I shouldn't expect them to, if they take a fancy to a common street boy. But when they find him out, they may change their opinion of you."

"I don't know how that will be, mother. At any rate, I think I ought to get more than four dollars a week where I am. Why, there's Talbot, only two years older than I, gets eight dollars, and I do more than he. To tell the truth, I don't like the place. I don't like to be seen carrying round bundles. It isn't fit work for a gentleman's son."

Roswell forgot that many of the most prosperous merchants in the city began in that way, only on less wages. One who wants to climb the ladder of success must, except in very rare cases, commence at the lowest round. This was what Roswell did not like. He wanted to begin half-way up at the very least. It was a great hindrance to him that he regarded himself as a gentleman's son, and was puffed up with a corresponding sense of his own importance.

The more Roswell thought of his ill-requited services, as he considered them, the more he felt aggrieved. It may be mentioned that he was employed in a dry goods store on Sixth Avenue, and was chiefly engaged in carrying out bundles for customers. A circumstance which occurred about this time deepened his disgust with the place.

About the middle of the next week he was carrying a heavy bundle to a house on Madison Avenue. Now it happened that Mr. Rockwell, who, it will be remembered, lived on the same street, had left home that morning, quite forgetting an important letter which he had received, and which required an early answer. He therefore summoned Dick, and said, "Richard, do you remember the location of my house?"

"Yes, sir," said Dick.

"I find I have left an important letter at home. I have written a line to my wife, that she may know where to look for it. I want you to go up at once."

"Very well, sir."

Dick took the note, and, walking to Broadway, jumped on board an omnibus, and in a few minutes found himself opposite the Fifth Avenue Hotel. Here he alighted, and, crossing the Park, entered Madison Avenue, then as now lined with fine houses.

Walking briskly up the avenue, he overtook a boy of about his own size, with a large bundle under his arm. Glancing at him as he passed, he recognized Roswell Crawford.

"How are you, Crawford?" said Dick, in an offhand manner.

Roswell looked at the speaker, whom he recognized.

"I'm well," said he, in a stiff, ungracious manner.

Ashamed of the large bundle he was carrying, he would rather have been seen by any boy than Dick, under present circumstances. He did not fail to notice Dick's neat dress, and the gold chain displayed on his vest. Indeed there was nothing in

Dick's appearance which would have been inconsistent with the idea that he lived on the avenue, and was, what Roswell claimed to be, a gentleman's son. It seemed to Roswell that Dick was immensely presumptuous in swaggering up Madison Avenue in such a style, as he mentally called it, and he formed the benevolent design of "taking down his pride," and making him feel uncomfortable, if possible.

"Have you lost your place?" he inquired.

"No," said Dick, "not yet. It's very kind of you to inquire."

"I suppose they pay you for walking the streets, then," he said, with a sneer.

"Yes," said Dick, composedly; "that's one of the things they pay me for."

"I suppose you like it better than blacking boots?" said Roswell, who, supposing that Dick was ashamed of his former occupation, felt a malicious pleasure in reminding him of it.

"Yes," said Dick, "I like it better on the whole; but then there's some advantages about boot-blackin'."

"Indeed!" said Roswell, superciliously. "As I was never in the business, I can't of course decide."

"Then I was in business for myself, you see, and was my own master. Now I have to work for another man."

"You don't seem to be working very hard now," said Roswell, enviously.

"Not very," said Dick. "You must be tired carrying that heavy bundle. I'll carry it for you as far as I go."

Roswell, who was not above accepting a favor from a boy he didn't like, willingly transferred it to our hero.

"I carried it out just to oblige," he said, as if he were not in the daily habit of carrying such packages.

"That's very kind of you," said Dick.

Roswell did not know whether Dick spoke sarcastically or not, and therefore left the remark unnoticed.

"I don't think I shall stay where I am very long," he said.

"Don't you like?" asked Dick.

"Not very well. I'm not obliged to work for a living," added Roswell, loftily, but not altogether truly.

"I am," said Dick. "I've had to work for a living ever since I was six years old. I suppose you work because you like it."

"I'm learning business. I'm going to be a merchant, as my father was."

"I'll have to give up the bundle now," said Dick. "This is as far as I am going."

Roswell took back his bundle, and Dick went up the steps of Mr. Rockwell's residence and rang the door-bell.

CHAPTER X.

A STORE ON SIXTH AVENUE.

Roswell kept on his way with his heavy bundle, more discontented than ever. The bundle seemed heavier than ever. Dick had no such bundles to carry. He had an easier time, his business position was better, and his wages more than double. And all this in spite of the glaring fact that Roswell was a gentleman's son, and Dick wasn't. Surely fortune was very blind, and unfair in the distribution of her favors.

"I suppose he'll be crowing over me," thought Roswell, bitterly, judging from what would have been his own feeling had the case been reversed. "I hope he'll have to go back to boot-blacking some day. I wish mother'd buy me a gold watch and chain. There'd be some sense in *my* wearing it."

Roswell evidently thought it very inappropriate that Dick should wear a handsome gold watch, more especially as he was quite sure beforehand that his mother would not gratify his own desire to possess one. Still he resolved to ask.

There was another thing he meant to ask. Feeling that his services were worth more than the wages he received, and convincing himself that his employers would be unwilling to lose him, he determined to ask an advance of two dollars a week, making six dollars in all. Not that he considered that even this would pay him, but as he could hardly hope that he would be appreciated according to his deserts, he limited his request to that sum. He concluded to defer making his application until Saturday evening, when he would receive his week's wages.

He consulted his mother upon this subject, and she, having nearly as high an opinion of her promising son as he had himself, consented to the application. If his cousin, James Gilbert, had heard of his intention, he was enough of a business man to have dissuaded him from the attempt. Though he saw fit to espouse the cause of Roswell against Dick, it was more because he disliked the latter than because he was blind to the faults of the former. Indeed, he had a very moderate opinion of his young cousin's capabilities.

The days slipped by, and Saturday night came. It was nine o'clock before Roswell was released, the Saturday-night trade being the best of the week. The other clerks had been paid, Roswell's turn coming last, because he was the youngest.

The designation of the firm was Hall & Turner. Mr. Hall, the senior partner, usually went home early in the evening; and Mr. Turner, the junior partner, a man of about thirty-five, attended to the evening business, and paid the weekly wages.

"Here, Crawford," he said, counting out four one dollar bills; "it's your turn now."

"I want to speak to you for a moment, Mr. Turner," said Roswell, beginning to feel a little nervous; for now that the time had come for making his request, he felt a little uncertain how it would be received.

"Very well," said his employer, showing a little surprise; "be quick about it, for I want to get through."

"I want to know if you will not be willing to raise my wages," said Roswell, rather awkwardly.

"On what ground do you ask for it?" said Mr. Turner, looking up.

"I thought I might be worth more," said Roswell.

"How long have you been in my employment,—do you remember?"

"About four months," said Roswell.

"Do you think you have learned enough in that time to make you worth more?"

"Yes, sir," said Roswell, with a little hesitation.

"How much more would satisfy you?"

"Two dollars more,—for the present," said Roswell, beginning to feel a little hopeful.

"That is six dollars a week."

"Yes, sir."

"And how soon would you expect another advance?" asked Mr. Turner, quietly.

"In about six months."

"You are quite moderate in your demands, certainly."

There was something in Mr. Turner's tone which struck Roswell as unfavorable, and he hastily said in his own justification:—

"There's a friend of mine, no older than I am, who gets ten dollars a week."

Certainly Roswell must have spoken inadvertently, or he would hardly have referred to Dick as his friend; but his main idea at present was to produce an impression upon the mind of Mr. Turner.

"Is your friend in a dry goods store?" asked Mr. Turner.

"No, sir."

"Then I don't see that his wages have any bearing upon your case. There may be some special circumstances that affect his compensation. How long has he been in the service of his present employer?"

"Only a week or two."

"Is this his first place?"

"Yes, sir."

"It may be that he is some relative of his employer."

"That isn't very likely," said Roswell, his lip curling. "He used to be a boot-black about the streets."

"Indeed!" said Mr. Turner, keenly. "I think you said he was a friend of yours."

"No, sir," said Roswell, proudly; "I haven't the honor."

"You certainly said 'There's a friend of mine, no older than I am, who gets ten dollars a week.'"

"I didn't mean to speak of him as my friend," said Roswell; "I'm a gentleman's son."

"If you are, his friendship might do you no harm. If he receives the wages you state, he must be a smart fellow. If he didn't earn as much, probably he would not receive it."

"I don't believe he'll keep his place long," muttered Roswell, his wish being father to the thought.

"If he doesn't, you may be able to succeed him," said Mr. Turner. "I shall be compelled to refuse your request. Indeed, so far from increasing your compensation, I have been considering during the last week whether it would not be for my interest to get another boy in your place."

"Sir!" exclaimed Roswell, in dismay.

"I will give you my reasons. You appear to think yourself of too great consequence to discharge properly the duties of your position."

"I don't understand you, sir," stammered Roswell.

"I believe you claim to be a gentleman's son."

"Yes, sir," said Roswell. "My father used to keep a store on Broadway."

"And I am led to suppose you think it incompatible with your dignity to carry bundles to different parts of the city."

"I would rather stand behind the counter and sell goods," said Roswell.

"Of course you will be a salesman in time, if you stick to business faithfully. But it so happens that we didn't hire you as a salesman, but as a boy, whose chief business it should be to carry bundles. But we don't want to impose a disagreeable duty upon you. Therefore, if you think upon reflection that you would prefer not to continue in your situation, we will hire somebody else."

"That won't be necessary, sir," said Roswell, considerably crest-fallen.

"You are content, then, to remain?"

"Yes, sir."

"And upon four dollars a week?"

"Yes, sir. I suppose I may hope to have my wages increased some time?"

"When we find your services worth more, you shall receive more," said Mr. Turner. "That is fair,—isn't it?"

"Yes, sir."

"Then here is your money. I didn't mean to talk so long; but it's as well to come to an understanding."

Roswell left the store considerably crest-fallen. He found that, instead of regarding him worth an advance of wages, Mr. Turner had had it in his mind to discharge him; and that hurt his pride. It was certainly very singular that people shouldn't be more impressed with the fact that he was a gentleman's son. He could not have received less deference if he had been an ex-boot-black, like Dick himself. He certainly was no more contented than before, nor was his self-appreciation materially diminished. If the world did not recognize his claims, there was one comfort, his mother appreciated him, and he appreciated himself. As to his cousin, he did not feel quite so certain.

"Why are you so late, Roswell?" asked his mother, looking up from her work as he entered. "It seems to me they kept you later than usual at the store, even for Saturday evening."

"I'm sick of the store," said Roswell, impatiently.

"What's the matter?"

"I asked old Turner to-night if he wouldn't raise my wages," said Roswell.

"Well, what did he say?"

"He said he wouldn't do it."

"Did he give any reason?"

"He said I didn't earn any more. He's a stingy old hunks, any way, and I wish I was in another place."

43

"So do I; but it isn't so easy to get a new position. You had better stay in this till another offers."

"I hate carrying bundles through the streets. It isn't fit work for a gentleman's son."

"Ah, if your poor father had lived, things would have been very different with us all!" said Mrs. Crawford, with a sigh. She chose to forget that previous to his death her late husband's habits had been such that he contributed very little to the comfort or support of the family.

"I wouldn't care if I were a salesman," continued Roswell; "but I don't like being an errand boy. I'd just as lives go to the post-office for letters, or to the bank with money, but, as for carrying big bundles of calico under my arm, I don't like it. I was walking on Madison Avenue the other day with a ten-pound bundle, when the boot-black came up, dressed handsomely, with a gold watch and chain, and exulted over me for carrying such a big bundle."

There was a little exaggeration about this, for Dick was very far from exulting over Roswell, otherwise he certainly would not have volunteered to carry the bundle himself. But it often happens that older persons than Roswell are not above a little misrepresentation now and then.

"He's an impudent fellow, then!" said Mrs. Crawford, indignantly. "Then Mr. Hall won't raise your wages?"

"It wasn't Mr. Hall I asked. It was Mr. Turner," said Roswell.

"Didn't he hold out any hopes of raising your wages hereafter?"

"He said he would raise them when I deserve it. He don't amount to much. He's no gentleman," said Roswell, scornfully.

"Who's no gentleman?" inquired James Gilbert, who chanced just then to enter the room.

"Mr. Turner."

"Who's Mr. Turner?"

"My employer,—Hall & Turner, you know."

"What's amiss with him?"

"I asked him to raise my wages to-night, and he wouldn't."

"Umph! How much did you ask for?"

"Two dollars more a week."

"You're a fool!"

"*What?*" said Roswell, astonished.

"What!" exclaimed Mrs. Crawford, angrily.

"I say the lad's a fool to ask for so large an advance so soon. Of course his employers refused it. I would, in their place."

"You're very hard upon the poor boy!" said Mrs. Crawford. "I thought you were his friend."

"So I am; but he's acted foolishly for all that. He should have known better."

"I ought to be worth six dollars, if your boot-black is worth ten," responded Roswell.

"He isn't worth ten."

"Why do you pay him that, then?"

"It's Mr. Rockwell who pays him, not I. Why he does it, I can't say. It isn't because he earns it. No boy of his age, or yours either, can earn ten dollars a week."

"At any rate he gets ten, and I get only four. I certainly earn more than that," said Roswell.

"I am not so sure about that," said his cousin. "But if it will afford you any comfort, I'll venture to make the prediction that he won't remain in Rockwell & Cooper's employment a week longer."

"Has anything happened?" asked Roswell, eagerly.

"*Not yet*," said James Gilbert, significantly.

"Then something is going to happen?"

"You need not trouble yourself to ask questions. Wait patiently, and when anything happens I'll let you know."

Here James Gilbert left the room, and went up to his own chamber. His words had excited hope in both Roswell and his mother. The former felt that it would be a satisfaction to him to learn that Dick had lost his situation, even if he failed to get it himself.

CHAPTER XI.

A NEW ALLIANCE.

The name of Micky Maguire is already familiar to the readers of "Ragged Dick." He had acquired a prominent position among the down-town boot-blacks by his strength, which he used oftentimes to impose upon boys weaker than himself. He was a young ruffian, indeed, with few redeeming qualities. When Dick was in the same business, he tried on two or three occasions to make him acknowledge his superiority; but it was not in Dick's nature to be subservient to any one whom he did not respect. Moreover, Dick had two good stout arms of his own, and knew how to use them in self-defence. The consequence was that Micky Maguire signally failed in the attempts which he made on different occasions to humble our hero, and was obliged to slink off in discomfiture with his satellite, Limpy Jim.

The last glimpse we had of Micky was in Dick's cast-off clothes, of which by some means, probably not honest, he had become possessed. He did not wear them long, however. The famous Washington coat and Napoleon pants were only mortal, and, being already of venerable antiquity, became at length too fragmentary even for Micky's not very fastidious taste. One morning, accordingly, having levied an unwilling contribution from a weaker but more industrious boot-black, Micky went to Baxter Street, and invested it in a blue coat with brass buttons, which, by some strange chain of circumstances, had found its way thither from some country town, where it may at one time have figured at trainings and on town-meeting days. A pair of overalls completed Micky's costume. He dispensed with a vest, his money not having been sufficient to buy that also.

Certainly Micky presented a noticeable figure as he stood in the City Hall Park, clad in the above-mentioned garments. He was rather proud of the brass buttons, and may even have fancied, in his uncultivated taste, that his new costume became him.

While he was swaggering about he espied part of a cigar, which some one had thrown aside. Micky, who was fond of smoking, picked it up, and looked about him for a light, not being provided with a match. A young man was slowly crossing the park with a cigar in his mouth. But he was evidently plunged in thought, and hardly conscious of the scene about him. Micky observed this, and a cunning scheme suggested itself.

He walked up to the young man, and said, cavalierly, "Give us a light, mister, will yer?"

The young man mechanically took the cigar from his mouth, and passed it to the questioner without observing who he was. Had he done so, it is doubtful whether the request would have been complied with.

Rapidly calculating that he would not notice the substitution, Micky, after lighting the "stub," handed it to the young man, retaining the good cigar himself, and placing it straightway in his mouth.

This trick would probably have passed off undetected, if it had not been observed by some of Micky's fellow-professionals.

A jeering laugh from these called the young man's attention to the substitution, and, with a look of indignation, he said, "You young rascal, you shall pay for this!"

But Micky evaded his grasp, and scudded rapidly through the park, pursued by the victim of misplaced confidence.

"Run, Micky; I'll bet on you!" cried Pat Nevins, encouragingly.

"Go it, long legs!" said another, who backed the opposite party. "Give him a good lickin' when you catch him."

"Maybe you'd have to wait too long for that," said Pat.

"Leave yer cigar wid us, mister," said another boy.

James Gilbert, for he was the young man in question, began to find that he was becoming rather ridiculous, and felt that he would rather let Micky go free than furnish a spectacle to the crowd of boot-blacks who were surveying the chase with eager interest. He accordingly stopped short, and, throwing down the "stub," prepared to leave the park.

"Don't give it up, mister! You'll catch him," said his first backer. "Micky can't run far. Ragged Dick give him a stretcher once."

"Ragged Dick!" said Gilbert, turning abruptly at the sound of this name.

"Maybe you know him?"

"Does he black boots?"

"He used to, but he don't now."

46

"What does he do?"

"Oh, he's a swell now, and wears good clothes."

"How is that?"

"He's in a store, and gets good pay."

"What's the name of the boy that ran away with my cigar?"

"Micky Maguire."

"Was he a friend of Ragged Dick, as you call him?"

"Not much. They had two or three fights."

"Which beat?"

"Dick. He can fight bully."

Gilbert felt disappointed. He was in hopes our hero had met with a defeat. Somehow he seemed born for success.

"Then I suppose Maguire hates him?"

"I'll bet he does."

"Humph!" thought Gilbert; "I may turn his enmity to some account. Let me consider a little."

At length a plan suggested itself, and his countenance cleared up, and assumed an expression of satisfaction. On reaching home he held the conversation with Roswell and his mother which has been recorded at the close of the last chapter.

Meantime Micky went home to a miserable lodging on Worth Street, in the precincts of the Five Points, and very near where the Five Points House of Industry now stands. This admirable institution has had a salutary influence, and contributed greatly to the improvement of the neighborhood. Then, however, it was about as vile and filthy as could well be.

Micky exulted not a little at the success of his cunning, and smoked the cigar— an expensive one, by the way—with not a little satisfaction. He recounted the story to a group of admiring friends who had not been fortunate enough to witness it.

"It's you that's got the cheek, Micky," said Teddy Donovan.

"You did it neat," said another. "Maybe I'll try that same, some day."

"You'd better not. The copp might get hold of you."

"Was it a good cigar, Micky?"

"Wasn't it, just! I wish I'd got another. Stand treat, Teddy."

"I would if I had the stamps. I'm savin' up my money to go to the Old Bowery to-night."

The boys were standing in a little group, and in the interest of their discussion did not observe the approach of James Gilbert, who was now visiting the park with a special object in view. With an expression of satisfaction he recognized the boy who had served him a trick the day before. Indeed, it was not easy to mistake Micky. The blue coat with brass buttons and the faded overalls would have betrayed him, even if his superior height had not distinguished him from his comrades.

Had Micky been aware of Gilbert's approach he would have thought it prudent to "change his base;" but, his back being turned, he was taken by surprise. His attention was drawn by a tap on the shoulder, and, looking round, he recognized his enemy, as he regarded him. He started to run, but was withheld by a strong grasp.

"Leave me alone, will yer?" he said, ducking his head as if he expected a blow.

"I believe you are fond of smoking," said Gilbert, continuing to hold him tight. Micky maintained silence.

"And sometimes exchange a poor cigar for a good one?" continued his captor.

"It was a mistake," said Micky.

"What did you run for, then?"

"What you going to do about it, mister?" asked one boy, curiously.

"So it was a mistake,—was it?" said Gilbert.

"Yes, sir," said Micky, glibly.

"Take care you don't make the mistake again, then. Now you may black my boots."

Not only the boys who were standing by, but Micky himself, were considerably surprised at this unexpected turn. They confidently expected that Micky would "get a lickin'," and instead of that, he had found a customer. Their respect for Gilbert was considerably diminished for failing to exact punishment, and, their interest in the affair being over, they withdrew.

Micky laid down his box, and commenced operations.

"How long have you been a boot-black?" asked Gilbert.

"Five years—goin' on six," said Micky.

"Can you earn much?"

"No," said Micky. "Business aint very good now."

"You manage to dress well," said Gilbert, with an amused look at Micky's habiliments.

"Yes," said Micky, with a glance at the brass buttons; "but I had to borrer the money to buy my clo'es."

"There used to be a boy around here that was called Dick. Did you know him?"

"There be a good many Dicks. Which did you mean?"

"This boy was nearly your size. I believe they called him 'Ragged Dick.'"

"I know'd him," said Micky, shortly, with a scowl.

"Was he a friend of yours?"

"No, he wasn't. I give him a lickin' once."

The fact happened to be the other way; but Micky was not very scrupulous as to the strict truth of his statements.

"You don't like him, then? Where is he now?"

"He's in a store, and swells round with good clothes."

"Have you seen him lately?"

"No, an' I don't want to."

"He wears a gold watch now. I suppose he wouldn't have anything to say to you."

"Maybe not," said Mickey.

"It would be a good joke if he should lose his place and have to go back to boot-blacking again."

"I wish he would," said Micky, fervently. "It 'ould cure him of puttin' on airs."

"If, for example, his employer should be convinced that he was a thief, he would discharge him."

48

"Do you know him, mister?" asked Micky, looking up suddenly.

"Yes."

"Is he a friend of yours?"

"I like him about as well as you do," said Gilbert.

"Done!" said Micky, releasing the second foot.

"Suppose you brush the other boot again. I'll pay you double. I want to talk to you a little."

"All right!" said Micky, and he resumed operations.

The conversation that followed we do not propose to chronicle. The results will appear hereafter. Enough that Gilbert and Micky departed mutually satisfied, the latter the richer by five times his usual fee.

CHAPTER XII.

DICK FALLS INTO A TRAP.

One evening, when Dick and Fosdick returned from their respective stores, a surprise awaited them.

"The postman left some letters for you," said the servant, as she opened the door to admit them.

"Maybe they're from the tax-collectors," said Dick. "That's the misfortun' of being men of property. What was your tax last year, Fosdick?"

"I don't remember such trifles," said Fosdick.

"I don't think they was taxes," said the girl, seriously; "they looked as if they was from a young lady."

"Very likely they are from Fosdick's wife," said Dick. "She's rusticatin' in the country for the benefit of her health."

"Maybe they're from yours, Mr. Hunter," said the girl, laughing.

"No," said Dick, gravely, "I'm a disconsolate widower, which accounts for my low spirits most of the time, and my poor appetite. Where are the letters?"

"I left them on the bureau in your room," said the servant. "They come this afternoon at three o'clock."

Both Fosdick and Dick felt not a little curious as to who could have written them letters, and hastened upstairs. Entering their chamber, they saw two very neat little notes, in perfumed French envelopes, and with the initial G in colors on the back. On opening them they read the following in a neat, feminine, fine handwriting. As both were alike, it will be sufficient to give Dick's.

"Miss Ida Greyson presents her compliments to Mr. Richard Hunter, and solicits the pleasure of his company on Thursday evening next, at a little birthday party.

"No. — *West Twenty-Fourth Street.*"

"We're getting fashionable," said Dick. "I didn't use to attend many parties when we lived in Mott Street and blacked boots for a livin'. I'm afraid I shan't know how to behave."

"I shall feel a little bashful," said Fosdick; "but I suppose we've got to begin some time."

"Of course," said Dick. "The important position we hold in society makes it necessary. How'll I be able to hold levees when I'm mayor, if I don't go into society now?"

"Very true," said Fosdick; "I don't expect to occupy any such position; but we ought to go in acknowledgment of Mr. Greyson's kindness."

Mr. Greyson was the teacher of the Sunday-school class of which both Dick and Fosdick were members. His recommendation had procured Fosdick his present place, and he had manifested his kindness in various ways. Those who have read "Ragged Dick" will remember that he had a very sprightly and engaging daughter of ten years of age, who seemed to have taken an especial fancy to Dick. Being wealthy, his kindness had been of great service to both boys, inspiring them with self-respect, and encouraging them to persevere in their efforts to raise themselves to a higher position.

The dinner-bell rang just as the boys had finished their discussion, and they went down and took places at the table.

Soon Miss Peyton came sailing in, shaking her ringlets coquettishly. She was proud of these ringlets, and was never tired of trying their fascinations upon gentlemen. But somehow they had not succeeded in winning a husband.

"Good-evening, Mr. Hunter," said she. "You look as if you had had good news."

"Do I?" said Dick. "Perhaps you can tell what it is."

"I know how it came," said Miss Peyton, significantly.

"Then I hope you won't keep me in suspense any longer than you can help."

"Perhaps you'd rather I wouldn't mention before company."

"Never mind," said Dick. "Don't have any regard to my feelin's. They're tough, and can stand a good deal."

"How do you like the letter G?" asked Miss Peyton, slyly.

"Very much," said Dick, "as long as it behaves itself. What is your favorite letter?"

"Don't think I'm going to tell you, Mr. Hunter. That was a pretty little note, and in a young lady's hand too."

"Yes," said Dick. "Perhaps you'd like to see it."

"You wouldn't show it to me on any account, I know."

"You may see it if you like," said Dick.

"May I, really? I should like to very much; but would the young lady like it?"

"I don't think she'd mind. She's written one to my friend Fosdick just like it."

Dick passed the invitation across the table.

"It's very pretty indeed," said Miss Peyton. "And is Miss Ida Greyson very handsome?"

"I'm no judge of beauty," said Dick.

"So she lives in West Twenty-Fourth Street. Is her father rich?"

"I don't know how rich," said Dick; "but my impression is that his taxes last year were more than mine."

"I know now what your favorite letters are," said Miss Peyton. "They are I. G."

"I. G. are very well as long as you don't put P. before them," said Dick. "Thank you for another cup of tea, Mrs. Browning."

"I should think you'd need some tea after such a brilliant effort, Hunter," said Mr. Clifton, from across the table.

"Yes," said Dick. "I find my brain gets exhausted every now and then by my intellectual efforts. Aint you troubled that way?"

"Can't say I am. Don't you want to go out and try a game of billiards this evening?"

"No, thank you. I've got to study."

"I expect to see you a college professor some of these days."

"I haven't made up my mind yet," said Dick. "I'm open to an offer, as the oyster remarked when he was placed on the table. If I can serve my fellow-men best by bein' a college professor, and gettin' a big salary, I'm willin' to sacrifice my private feelin's for the public good."

"Do you agree with your friend, Mr. Fosdick?" said Miss Peyton. "Won't you favor us with your views?"

"I have none worth mentioning," said Fosdick. "I leave my friend to do the talking, while I attend to the eating."

"Mr. Hunter's remarks are very entertaining," said Miss Peyton.

"Thank you," said Dick; "but my friend prefers a different kind of entertainment."

The boys rose from the table, and went up to their room to look over the evening's lessons. They were quite pleased with their new teacher, whom they found not only competent for his task, but interested in promoting their progress. He was able to help them readily out of their difficulties, and encouraged them to persevere. So they came to look forward to their evening lessons not as tasks, but as pleasant exercises.

"It's strange," said Dick, one evening after the teacher had left them; "I used to enjoy goin' to the Old Bowery so much. I went two or three times a week sometimes. Now I would a good deal rather stay at home and study."

"Then you didn't have a home, and the lighted theatre must have been much pleasanter than the cold and cheerless streets."

"Yes, that was it. I used to get so tired sometimes of having no home to go to, and nobody to speak to that I cared about."

"You'd hardly like to go back to the old life, Dick?"

"No, it would come pretty hard to me now. I didn't seem to mind it so much then."

"Because you had never known anything better."

"No. It was a lucky day when I met you, Fosdick. I'd never have had the patience to learn. Readin', or tryin' to read, always gave me the headache."

51

"You always leave off the last letter in such words as 'reading,' Dick. You should be more careful, now that you associate with educated persons."

"I know it, Fosdick, but I'm so used to droppin'—I mean dropping—the g that it comes natural. I will try to remember it. But about this party,—shall we have to get new clothes?"

"No, we have each a nice suit, and we shan't be expected to dress in the height of the fashion."

"I wish it was over. I dread it."

"So do I a little; but I think we shall enjoy it. Ida is a nice girl."

"That's so. If I had a sister I'd like her to be like Ida."

"Perhaps she'd like a brother like you. I notice she seems to fancy your company."

"I hope you're not jealous, Fosdick. You can be a brother to Miss Peyton, you know."

Fosdick laughed. "There's no chance for me there either," he said. "She evidently prefers you."

"I'll adopt her for my aunt if it'll be gratifying to her feelings," said Dick; "but I aint partial to ringlets as a general thing."

It is well perhaps that Miss Peyton did not hear these remarks, as she cherished the idea that both Fosdick and Dick were particularly pleased with her.

A day or two afterwards Dick was walking leisurely through Chatham Street, about half past one o'clock. He was allowed an hour, about noon, to go out and get some lunch, and he was now on his way from the restaurant which he usually frequented. As it was yet early, he paused before a window to look at something which attracted his attention. While standing here he became conscious of a commotion in his immediate neighborhood. Then he felt a hand thrust into the side-pocket of his coat, and instantly withdrawn. Looking up, he saw Micky Maguire dodging round the corner. He put his hand into his pocket mechanically, and drew out a pocket-book.

Just then a stout, red-faced man came up puffing, and evidently in no little excitement.

"Seize that boy!" he gasped, pointing to Dick. "He's got my pocket-book."

Contrary to the usual rule in such cases, a policeman did happen to be about, and, following directions, stepped up, and laid his hand on Dick's shoulder.

"You must go with me, my fine fellow," he said "Hand over that pocket-book, if you please."

"What's all this about?" said Dick. "Here's the pocket-book, if it is yours. I'm sure I don't want it."

"You're a cool hand," said the guardian of the public peace. "If you don't want it, what made you steal it from this gentleman's pocket?"

"I didn't take it," said Dick, shortly.

"Is this the boy that stole your pocket-book?" demanded the policeman of the red-faced man, who had now recovered his breath.

"It's the very young rascal. Does he pretend to deny it?"

"Of course he does. They always do."

"When it was found on him too! I never knew such barefaced impudence."

"Stop a minute," said Dick, "while I explain. I was standing looking in at that window, when I felt something thrust into my pocket. I took it out and found it to be that pocket-book. Just then that gentleman came up, and charged me with the theft."

"That's a likely story," said the officer. "If any one put the pocket-book into your pocket, it shows you were a confederate of his. You'll have to come with me."

And poor Dick, for the first time in his life, was marched to the station-house, followed by his accuser, and a gang of boys. Among these last, but managing to keep at a respectful distance, was Micky Maguire.

CHAPTER XIII.

DICK IN THE STATION-HOUSE.

Poor Dick! If Trinity Church spire had suddenly fallen to the ground, it could scarcely have surprised and startled him more than his own arrest for theft.

During the hard apprenticeship which he had served as a street boy, he had not been without his share of faults and errors; but he had never, even under the severest pressure, taken what did not belong to him.

Of religious and moral instruction he had then received none; but something told him that it was mean to steal, and he was true to this instinctive feeling. Yet, if he had been arrested a year before, it would have brought him less shame and humiliation than now. Now he was beginning to enjoy the feeling of respectability, which he had compassed by his own earnest efforts. He felt he was regarded with favor by those whose good opinion was worth having, and his heart swelled within him as he thought that they might be led to believe him guilty. He had never felt so down-hearted as when he walked in company with the policeman to the station-house, to be locked up for examination the next morning.

"You wasn't sharp enough this time, young fellow," said the policeman.

"Do you think I stole the pocket-book?" asked Dick, looking up in the officer's face.

"Oh, no, of course not! You wouldn't do anything of that kind," said the policeman, ironically.

"No, I wouldn't," said Dick, emphatically. "I've been poor enough and hungry enough sometimes, but I never stole. It's mean."

"What is your name?" said the officer. "I think I have seen you before."

"I used to black boots. Then my name was Ragged Dick. I know you. Your name is Jones."

"Ragged Dick! Yes, yes, I remember. You used to be pretty well out at elbows, if I remember rightly."

"My clothes used to be pretty well ventilated," said Dick, smiling faintly. "That was what made me so healthy, I expect. But did you ever know me to steal?"

"No," said the officer, "I can't say I have."

"I lived about the streets for more then eight years," said Dick, "and this is the first time I was ever arrested."

"What do you do now?"

"I'm in a store on Pearl Street."

"What wages do you get?"

"Ten dollars a week."

"Do you expect me to believe that story?"

"It's true."

"I don't believe there's a boy of your age in the city that gets such wages. You can't earn that amount."

"I jumped into the water, and saved the life of Mr. Rockwell's little boy. That's why he pays me so much."

"Where did you get that watch and chain? Are they gold?"

"Yes, Mrs. Rockwell gave them to me."

"It seems to me you're in luck."

"I wasn't very lucky to fall in with you," said Dick. "Don't you see what a fool I should be to begin to pick pockets now when I am so well off?"

"That's true," said the officer, who began to be shaken in his previous conviction of Dick's guilt.

"If I'd been going into that business, I would have tried it when I was poor and ragged. I should not have waited till now."

"If you didn't take the pocket-book, then how came it in your pocket?"

"I was looking in at a shop window, when I felt it thrust into my pocket. I suppose it was the thief who did it, to get out of the scrape himself."

"That might be. At any rate, I've known of such cases. If so, you are unlucky, and I am sorry for you. I can't let you go, because appearances are against you, but if there is anything I can do to help you I will."

"Thank you, Mr. Jones," said Dick, gratefully. "I did not want you to think me guilty. Where is the man that lost the pocket-book?"

"Just behind us."

"I should like to speak to him a moment."

The red-faced man, who was a little behind, came up, and Dick asked, quietly, "What makes you think I took your pocket-book, sir?"

"Wasn't it found in your pocket, you young rascal?" said the other, irritably.

"Yes," said Dick.

"And isn't that enough?"

"Not if somebody else put it there," said Dick.

"That's a likely story."

"It's a true story."

"Can you identify this as the boy who robbed you, and whom you saw running?"

54

"No," said the red-faced man, rather unwillingly. "My eyesight is not very good, but I've no doubt this is the young rascal."

"Well, that must be decided. You must appear to-morrow morning to prefer your complaint."

"Mind you don't let the rascal escape," said the other.

"I shall carry him to the station-house, where he will be safe."

"That's right, I'll make an example of him. He won't pick my pocket again in a hurry."

"I hope the judge won't be so sure that I am guilty," said Dick. "If he is, it'll go hard with me."

"Why don't you call your employer to testify to your good character?"

"That's a good idea. Can I write a note to him, and to another friend?"

"Yes; but perhaps the mail wouldn't carry them in time."

"I will send a messenger. Can I do so?"

"When we get to the station-house I will see that you have a chance to send. Here we are."

Escorted by the officer, and followed by his accuser, Dick entered. There was a railing at the upper end of the room, and behind it a desk at which sat a captain of the squad.

The officer made his report, which, though fair and impartial, still was sufficient to cause our hero's commitment for trial.

"What is your name?" questioned the captain.

Dick thought it best to be straightforward, and, though he winced at the idea of his name appearing in the daily papers, answered in a manly tone, "Richard Hunter."

"Of what nation?"

"American."

"Where were you born?"

"In this city."

"What is your age?"

"Sixteen years."

These answers were recorded, and, as Dick expressed a desire to communicate with his friends before trial, permission was given him to write to them, and the trial was appointed for the next morning at the Tombs. The red-faced man certified that his wallet contained nine dollars and sixty-two cents, which was found to be correct. He agreed to be present the next morning to prefer his charge, and with such manifest pleasure that he was not retained, as it sometimes happens, to insure his appearance.

"I will find a messenger to carry your notes," said the friendly officer.

"Thank you," said Dick. "I will take care that you are paid for your trouble."

"I require no pay except what I have to pay the messenger."

Dick was escorted to a cell for safe-keeping. He quickly dashed off a letter to Mr. Murdock, fearing that Mr. Rockwell might not be in the store. It was as follows:—

"Mr. Murdock,—What will you think when I tell you that I have been unlucky enough to be arrested on suspicion of picking a man's pocket? The real thief slipped the wallet into my pocket as I was looking into a shop window, and it was found on me. I couldn't prove my innocence, so here I am at the station-house. They will think strange at the store because I am absent. Will you tell Mr. Rockwell privately what has detained me; but don't tell Mr. Gilbert. He don't like me any too well, and would believe me guilty at once, or pretend he did. I am sure *you* won't believe I would do such a thing, or Mr. Rockwell either. Will you come and see me to-night? I am to be tried to-morrow morning. I aint very proud of the hotel where I am stopping, but they didn't give me much choice in the matter.

"Richard Hunter."

"*Station-House, Franklin Street.*"

The other letter was to Fosdick; here it is:—

"Dear Fosdick,—I didn't much think when I left you this morning that I should be writing to you from the station-house before night. I'll tell you how it happened." [Here follows a detailed account, which is omitted, as the reader is already acquainted with all the circumstances.] "Of course they will wonder at the boarding-house where I am. If Miss Peyton or Mr. Clifton inquires after me to-night, you can say that I am detained by business of importance. That's true enough. I wish it wasn't. As soon as dinner is over, I wish you'd come and see me. I don't know if you can, not being acquainted with the rules of this hotel. I shan't stop here again very soon, if I can help it. There's a woman in the next cell, who was arrested for fighting. She is swearing frightfully. It almost makes me sick to be in such a place. It's pretty hard to have this happen to me just when I was getting along so well. But I hope it'll all come out right. Your true friend,

"Dick.

"P.S.—I've given my watch and chain to the officer to keep for me. Gold watches aint fashionable here, and I didn't want them to think me putting on airs.

"*Station-House, Franklin Street.*"

After Dick had written these letters he was left to himself. His reflections, as may readily be supposed, were not the most pleasant. What would they think at the boarding-house, if they should find what kind of business it was that had detained him! Even if he was acquitted, some might suppose that he was really guilty. But there was a worse contingency. He might be unable to prove his innocence, and might be found guilty. In that case he would be sent to the Island. Dick shuddered at the thought. Just when he began to feel himself respectable, it was certainly bad to meet with such hard luck. What, too, would Mr. Greyson and Ida think? He had been so constant at the Sunday school that his absence would be sure to be noticed, and he knew that his former mode of life would make his guilt more readily believed in the present instance.

"If Ida should think me a pick-pocket!" thought poor Dick, and the thought made him miserable enough. The fact was, that Ida, by her vivacity and lively manners, and her evident partiality for his society, had quite won upon Dick, who considered her by all odds the nicest girl he had ever seen. I don't mean to say that Dick was in love,—at least not yet. Both he and Ida were too young for that; but he was certainly quite an admirer of the young lady. Again, if he were convicted, he would have to give up the party to which he had been invited, and he could never hope to get another invitation.

All these reflections helped to increase Dick's unhappiness. I doubt if he had ever felt so unhappy in all his life. But it never once occurred to him that his arrest was brought about by the machinations of his enemies. He hadn't chanced to see Micky Maguire, and had no suspicion that it was he who dropped the wallet into his pocket. Still less did he suspect that Gilbert's hostility had led him so far as to conspire with such a boy as Micky against him. It was lucky that he did not know this, or he would have felt still more unhappy.

But it is now time to turn to Micky Maguire and Mr. Gilbert, whose joint scheme had met with so much success.

CHAPTER XIV.

MICKY MAGUIRE'S DISAPPOINTMENT.

Micky Maguire waited until Dick was actually on the way to the station-house, and then started for Pearl Street to acquaint Gilbert with the success of his machinations. His breast swelled with triumph at the advantage he had gained over his enemy.

"May be he'll keep his 'cheerin' reflections' to himself another time," thought Micky. "He won't have much to say about my going to the Island when he's been there himself. They won't stand none of his airs there, I'm thinkin'."

There was another pleasant aspect to the affair. Micky had not only triumphed over his enemy, but he was going to be paid for it. This was the stipulation between Gilbert and himself. The book-keeper had not promised any definite sum, but Micky, in speculating upon the proper compensation for his service, fixed upon five dollars as about what he ought to receive. Like many others who count their chickens before they are hatched, he had already begun to consider what he would buy with it when he had got it.

Now, only the day previous, Micky had noticed hanging in a window in Chatham Street, a silver watch, and chain attached, which was labelled "Genuine Silver, only Five Dollars." Since Micky had been the possessor of a blue coat with brass buttons, his thoughts had dwelt more than ever before on his personal appearance, and the watch had struck his fancy. He did not reflect much on the probable quality of a silver watch which could be sold for five dollars, and a chain thrown into the bargain. It was a watch, at any rate, and would make a show. Besides, Dick wore a watch, and Micky felt that he did not wish to be outdone. As soon as he received his reward he meant to go and buy it.

It was therefore in a very cheerful frame of mind that Micky walked up in front of Rockwell & Cooper's store, and took his stand, occasionally glancing at the window.

Ten minutes passed away, and still he remained unnoticed. He grew impatient, and determined to enter, making his business an excuse.

Entering, he saw through the open door of the office, the book-keeper, bending over the desk writing.

"Shine yer boots?" he asked.

Gilbert was about to answer angrily in the negative, when looking up he recognized his young confederate. His manner changed, and he said, "Yes, I believe I'll have a shine; but you must be quick about it."

Micky swung his box from his shoulder, and, sinking upon his knees, seized his brush, and went to work scientifically.

"Any news?" asked Gilbert, in a low voice.

"Yes, mister, I've done it," said Micky.

"Have you managed to trap him?"

"Yes, I left him on his way to the station-house."

"How did you manage it?"

"I grabbed an old fellow's wallet, and dropped it into Dick's pocket. He pulled it out, and while he was lookin' at it, up came the 'copp' and nabbed him."

"How about the man from whom the wallet was taken?"

"He came up puffin', and swore Dick was the chap that stole it."

"So he was carried off to the station-house?"

"Yes; he's there safe enough."

"Then we shall have to carry on business without him," said Gilbert, coolly. "I hope he will enjoy himself at his new quarters."

"Maybe they'll send him to the Island," said Micky, beginning his professional operations upon the second boot.

"Very likely," said Gilbert. "I suppose you've been there before this."

"Wot if I have?" said Micky, in rather a surly tone, for he did not relish the allusion.

"No offence," said Gilbert. "I only meant that if you have ever been there, you can judge whether your friend Dick will enjoy it."

"Not a great deal," said Micky; "but you needn't call him my friend. I hate him."

"Your enemy, then. But get through as soon as possible."

Micky struck his brush upon the floor to indicate that the job was finished, and, rising, waited for his fee.

Gilbert took from his pocket ten cents and handed him.

"That's for the shine," he said; "and here's something for the other matter."

So saying, he placed in the hand of the boot-black a bank-note.

Micky glanced at it, and his countenance changed ominously, when he perceived the denomination. It was a one-dollar bill!

"It's one dollar," he said.

"Isn't that enough?"

"No, it isn't," he answered, sullenly. "I might 'ave been nabbed myself. I can't afford to work on no such terms."

Micky was right. It certainly was a very small sum to receive for taking such a risk, apart from all moral considerations, and his dissatisfaction can hardly be wondered at. But Gilbert was not of a generous nature. In fact he was disposed to be mean, and in the present instance he had even expected to get the credit of being generous. A dollar, he thought, must seem an immense sum to a ragged boot-black. But Micky thought differently, and Gilbert felt irritated at his ingratitude.

"It's all you'll get," said he, roughly.

"Then you'd better get somebody else to do your dirty work next time, mister," said Micky, angrily.

"Clear out, you young blackguard!" exclaimed Gilbert, his temper by this time fully aroused. "Clear out, if you don't want to be kicked out!"

"Maybe you'll wish you'd given me more," said Micky, sullenly picking up his box, and leaving the office.

"What's the matter?" asked Mr. Murdock, who happened to come up just as Micky went into the street, and heard the last words of the altercation.

"Oh," said Gilbert, carelessly, "he wasn't satisfied with his pay. I gave him ten cents, but the young rascal wanted more."

As he said this, he turned back to his desk.

"I wonder whether Gilbert's going anywhere," thought the head clerk. "I never knew him so extravagant before. He must be going out this evening."

Just then it occurred to him that Dick had been absent longer than usual, and, as he needed his services, he asked, "Has Richard returned, Mr. Gilbert?"

"I haven't seen him."

"Did he go out at the usual time?"

"Yes."

"What can have detained him?" said Mr. Murdock, thoughtfully.

"He's probably fallen in with some of his old friends, and forgotten all about his duties."

"That is not his way," said Mr. Murdock, quietly, as he walked away. He understood very well Mr. Gilbert's hostility to Dick, and that the latter was not likely to receive a very favorable judgment at his hands.

Five minutes later a boy entered the store, and, looking about him a moment in uncertainty, said, "I want to see Mr. Murdock."

"I am Mr. Murdock," he answered.

"Then this note is for you."

The clerk felt instinctively that the note was from Dick, and, not wishing Gilbert to hear the conversation, motioned the boy to follow him to the back part of the store.

Then he opened and read the note quickly.

"Did Richard Hunter give this to you?" he asked.

"No," said Tim Ryan, for that was his name. "It was the 'copp' that arrested him."

"I suppose a 'copp' is a policeman."

"Yes, sir."

"Were you present when he was arrested?"

"Yes, sir."

"Do you know anything about it?"

"Yes, I seed it all."

"You saw the wallet taken?"

"Yes, sir."

"Did Richard take it?"

"You mean Dick?" said Tim, interrogatively, for Richard was to him a strange name.

"No, he didn't, then. He wouldn't steal. I never know'd him to."

"Then you know Dick?"

"Yes, sir. I've knowed him ever since I was so high," indicating a point about three feet above the floor.

"Then who did take it, if not he?"

"Micky Maguire."

"Who is he?"

"He blacks boots."

"Then how did it happen that he was not arrested?"

"Micky was smart enough to drop the wallet into Dick's pocket as he was standin' before a shop winder. Then he got out of the way, and Dick was nabbed by the 'copp.'"

"Is this Micky of whom you speak a friend of yours?"

"No; he likes to bully small boys."

"Then why didn't you tell the officer he had arrested the wrong boy?"

"I wanted to," said Tim, "for Dick's always been kind to me; but I was afraid Micky would give me a beatin' when he got free. Then there was another reason."

"What was that?"

"It's mean to tell of a fellow."

"Isn't it meaner to let an innocent boy get punished, when you might save him by telling?"

"Maybe it is," said Tim, perplexed.

"My lad," continued Mr. Murdock, "you say Dick has been kind to you. You now have an opportunity to repay all he has ever done, by clearing him from this false charge, which you can easily do."

"I'll do it," said Tim, stoutly. "I don't care if Micky does lick me for it."

"By the way," said Mr. Murdock, with a sudden thought, "what is the appearance of this Micky Maguire?"

"He's rather stout, and has freckles."

"Does he wear a blue coat, with large brass buttons?"

"Yes," said Tim, in surprise. "Do you know him?"

"I have seen him this morning," said Mr. Murdock. "Wait a minute, and I will give you a line to Dick; or rather it will not be necessary. If you can get a chance, let him know that I am going to call on him this afternoon. Will you be at the station-house, or near it, at six o'clock?"

"Yes, sir."

"Then we can arrange about your appearing as a witness at the trial. Here is half a dollar for your trouble in bringing the note."

"I don't want it, sir," said Tim. "I don't want to take anything for doing a good turn to Dick."

"But you have been prevented from earning money. You had better take it."

But Tim, who was a warm-hearted Irish boy, steadfastly refused, and left the store in quest of Henderson's hat and cap store, having also a note to deliver to Fosdick.

"So that was Micky Maguire who was here a little while since," said Mr. Murdock to himself. "It seems singular that immediately after getting Richard into trouble, he should have come here where he was employed. Can it be that Gilbert had a previous acquaintance with him?"

The more Mr. Murdock reflected, the more perplexed he became. It did cross his mind that the two might be in league against Dick; but then, on the other hand, they evidently parted on bad terms, and this seemed to make such a combination improbable. So he gave up puzzling himself about it, reflecting that time would clear up what seemed mysterious about the affair.

Gilbert, on his part, could not help wondering on what errand Tim Ryan came to Mr. Murdock. He suspected he might be a messenger from Dick, but thought it best not to inquire, and Mr. Murdock did not volunteer any information. When the store closed, the head clerk bent his steps towards the station-house.

CHAPTER XV.

THE FRANKLIN STREET STATION-HOUSE.

The station-house to which Dick had been conveyed is situated in that part of Franklin Street which lies between Centre and Baxter Streets. The last is one of the most wretched streets in the city, lined with miserable tenement houses, policy shops, and second-hand clothing stores. Whoever passes through it in the evening, will do well to look to the safety of his pocket-book and watch, if he is imprudent enough to carry either in a district where the Ten Commandments are unknown, or unregarded.

The station-house is an exception to the prevailing squalidness, being kept with great neatness. Mr. Murdock ascended the steps, and found himself in a large room, one side of which was fenced off by a railing. Behind this was a desk, at which sat the officer in charge. To him, Mr. Murdock directed himself.

"Have you a boy, named Richard Hunter, in the house?"

"Yes," said the sergeant, referring to his minutes. "He was brought in this afternoon, charged with picking a gentleman's pocket."

"There is some mistake about this. He is as honest as I am."

"I have nothing to do with that. He will have a fair trial to-morrow morning. All I have to do is to keep him in safe custody till then."

"Of course. Where is he?"

"In a cell below."

"Can I see him?"

"If you wish."

The officer summoned an attendant, and briefly ordered him to conduct Mr. Murdock to Dick's cell.

"This way, sir," said the attendant.

Mr. Murdock followed him through a large rear room, which is intended for the accommodation of the officers. Then, descending some steps into the courtyard, he descended thence into the apartments in the basement. Here are the cells for the temporary detention of offenders who are not at once sent to the Tombs for trial. The passages are whitewashed and the cells look very neat. They are on either side, with a grating, so that one passing along can look into them readily. They are probably about seven feet long, by four or five in width. A narrow raised bedstead, covered with a pallet, occupies one side, on which the prisoner can either lie or sit, as he pleases.

"How are you, boss?" asked a negro woman, who had been arrested for drunkenness, swaying forward, as Mr. Murdock passed, and nearly losing her balance as she did so. "Can't you give me a few cents to buy some supper?"

Turning from this revolting spectacle, Mr. Murdock followed his guide to the second cell beyond where our hero was confined.

"Is it you, Mr. Murdock?" exclaimed our hero, joyfully jumping to his feet. "I am glad to see you."

"And I am glad to see you; but I wish it were somewhere else," said Mr. Murdock.

"So do I," said Dick. "I aint partial to this hotel, though the accommodations is gratooitous, and the company is very select."

"I see you will have your joke, Dick, even in such a place."

"I don't feel so jolly as I might," said Dick. "I never was in the station-house before; but I shall be lucky if I don't get sent to a worse place."

"Have you any idea who took the wallet which was found in your pocket?"

"No," said Dick.

"Do you know a boy called Micky Maguire?" proceeded Mr. Murdock.

"Yes," said Dick, looking up in surprise. "Micky used to be a great friend of mine. He'd be delighted if he only knew that I was enjoyin' the hospitality of the government."

"He does know it," said Mr. Murdock, quietly.

"How do you know?" asked Dick, quickly.

"Because it was he that stole the wallet and put it in your pocket."

"How did you find out?" asked Dick, eagerly.

"Do you know a boy named Tim Ryan?"

"Yes; he's a good boy."

"It was he that brought me your note. He saw the whole proceeding."

62

"Why didn't he tell, and stop my bein' arrested, then?"

"I asked him that; but he said he was afraid Micky would beat him when he found out. But he is a friend of yours, and he stands ready to testify what he knows, at your trial, to-morrow morning."

"That's lucky," said Dick, breathing a sigh of relief. "So it was Micky that served me the trick. He always loved me like a brother, Micky did, but I didn't expect he'd steal for my benefit. I'm very much obliged to him, but I'd rather dispense with such little favors another time."

"You will be surprised to learn that Micky came round to our store this afternoon."

"What for?" questioned Dick, in amazement.

"I don't know whether he came by accident or design; but Mr. Gilbert employed him to black his boots."

"Mr. Gilbert!"

"Yes. They seemed to be conversing earnestly; but I was too far off to hear what was said. Finally, Gilbert appeared to get angry, and drove the boy out."

"That's strange!" said Dick, thoughtfully. "Mr. Gilbert loves me about as much as Micky does."

"Yes, there seems to be some mystery about it. We may find out some time what it is. But here is your friend Fosdick."

"How are you, Fosdick?" hailed Dick from his cell. "I'm holdin' a little levee down here. Did you receive my card of invitation?"

"I've been uneasy all the afternoon, Dick," said Fosdick. "Ever since I heard that you were here, I've been longing to come and see you."

"Then you aint ashamed of me, even if I am in the station-house?"

"Of course I know you don't deserve to be here. Tell me all about it. I only got a chance to speak a minute with Tim Ryan, for there were customers waiting."

"I'll tell you all I know myself," said Dick. "I'm sorry to keep you standing, but the door is locked, and I've accidentally lost the key. So I can't invite you into my parlor, as the spider invited the fly."

"Don't stand on ceremony, Dick. I'd just as lieves stay outside."

"So would I," said Dick, rather ruefully.

The story was told over again, with such new light as Mr. Murdock had been able to throw upon it.

"It's just like Micky," said Fosdick. "He's a bad fellow."

"It was rather a mean trick," said Dick; "but he hasn't had a very good bringin' up, or maybe he'd be a better boy."

That he should have spoken thus, at the moment when he was suffering from Micky's malice, showed a generosity of feeling which was characteristic of Dick. No one was more frank, open, or free from malice than he, though always ready to stand up for his rights when he considered them assailed. It is this quality in Dick, joined to his manly spirit, which makes him a favorite with me, as he is also with you, let me hope, young reader.

"It'll come out right, Dick," said Fosdick, cheerfully. "Tim Ryan's testimony will clear you. I feel a good deal better about it now than I did this afternoon, when I didn't know how things were likely to go with you."

"I hope so," said Dick. "But I'm afraid you won't get any supper, if you stay any longer with me."

"How about your supper, Dick?" asked Fosdick, with sudden thought. "Do they give you any in this establishment?"

"No," said Dick; "this hotel's on the European system, with improvements. You get your lodgin' for nothing, and nothing to eat along with it. I don't like the system much. I don't think I could stand it more'n a week without its hurtin' my constitution."

"I'll go out and get you something, Dick," said Fosdick, "if the rules of the establishment allow it. Shall I?"

"Well," said Dick, "I think I might eat a little, though the place isn't very stimulatin' to the appetite."

"What shall I bring you?"

"I aint particular," said Dick.

Just then the attendant came along, and Fosdick inquired if he would be allowed to bring his friend something to eat.

"Certainly," was the reply. "We provide nothing ourselves, as the prisoners only stay with us a few hours."

"I'll be right back," said Fosdick.

Not far from the station-house, Fosdick found a baker's shop, where he bought some bread and cakes, with which he started to return. As he was nearing the station-house, he caught sight of Micky Maguire hovering about the door. Micky smiled significantly as he saw Fosdick and his burden.

"Where are you carryin' that?" he asked.

"Why do you ask?" said Fosdick, who could not feel very friendly to the author of Dick's misfortune.

"Never mind why," said Micky. "I know well enough. It's for your friend Dick. How does he like his new lodgins'?"

"How do you like them? You've been there often enough."

"Don't be impudent, or I'll lam' ye," said Micky, scowling.

As Fosdick was considerably smaller than himself, Micky might have ventured upon an assault, but deemed it imprudent in the immediate vicinity of the station-house.

"Give my compliments to Dick," he said. "I hope he'll sleep well." '

To this Fosdick returned no answer, but, entering the building, descended to Dick's temporary quarters. He passed the bread and cake through the grating, and Dick, cheered by the hope of an acquittal on the morrow, and a speedy recovery of his freedom, partook with a good appetite.

"Can't you give me a mouthful, boss?" muttered the negro woman before mentioned, as she caught sight of Fosdick's load.

He passed a cake through the grating, which she seized eagerly, and devoured with appetite.

"I think I must be going," said Mr. Murdock, consulting his watch, "or my wife and children won't know what has become of me."

"Good-night, Mr. Murdock," said Dick. "Thank you for your kindness."

"Good-night, Richard. Keep up your courage."

"I'll try to."

Fosdick stopped longer. At last he went away, and our hero, left to himself, lay down upon his pallet and tried to get to sleep.

CHAPTER XVI.

ROSWELL CRAWFORD RETIRES FROM BUSINESS.

"Can you send this home for me?" asked a lady in Hall & Turner's store about three o'clock in the afternoon of the day on which Dick, as we have related, was arrested.

"Certainly, madam. Where shall it be sent?" asked the clerk.

"No. 47 West Fortieth Street," was the reply.

"Very well, it shall be sent up immediately. Here, Roswell."

Roswell Crawford came forward not very willingly. He had no great liking for the task which he saw would be required of him. Fortieth Street was at least a mile and a half distant, and he had already just returned from a walk in a different direction. Besides, the bundle was a large one, containing three dress patterns. He did not think it very suitable for a gentleman's son to be seen carrying such a large bundle through the streets.

"Why don't you send Edward?" he said, complainingly. "He doesn't do half as much as I."

"I shall send whom I please," said the clerk, sharply. "You wouldn't do anything if you could help it."

"I won't carry bundles much longer," said Roswell. "You put all the heaviest bundles off upon me."

Roswell's back being turned, he did not observe Mr. Turner, who had come up as he was speaking.

"What are you complaining about?" asked that gentleman.

Roswell turned, and colored a little when he saw his employer.

"What is the matter?" repeated Mr. Turner.

"Mr. Evans always gives me the largest bundles to carry," said Roswell.

"He is always complaining of having to carry bundles," said the clerk. "He says it isn't suitable work for a gentleman's son."

"I have noticed it," said Mr. Turner. "On the whole, I think, Mr. Crawford," he said, with mock deference, "I think you have mistaken your vocation in entering a

65

dry-goods store. I advise you to seek some more gentlemanly employment. At the end of the week, you are at liberty to leave my employment for one better suited to you."

"I'm ready to go now," said Roswell, sulkily.

"Very well; if you desire it, I will not insist upon your remaining. If you will come up to the desk, you shall receive what is due you."

It was somewhat humiliating to Roswell to feel that his services were so readily dispensed with. Still he had never liked the place, and heartily disliked carrying bundles. By going at once, he would get rid of the large bundle to be carried to West Fortieth Street. Congratulating himself, therefore, on the whole, on escaping from what he regarded as a degrading servitude, he walked up to the desk in a dignified manner, and received the wages due him.

"I hope you will find some more congenial employment," said Mr. Turner, who paid him the amount of his wages.

"I have no doubt I shall," said Roswell, loftily. "My father was a gentleman, and our family has considerable influence."

"Well, I wish you success. Good-by."

"Good-by," said Roswell, and walked out of the shop with head erect.

He did not quite like going home at once, as explanation would be rather awkward under the circumstances. He accordingly crossed over to Fifth Avenue, considering that the most suitable promenade for a gentleman's son. He could not help regarding with some envy the happy possessors of the elegant buildings which he passed. Why had partial Fate denied him that fortune which would have enabled him to live in this favored locality?

"Plenty of snobs have got money," he thought. "How much better I could use it than they! I wish I were rich! You wouldn't catch me slaving my life out in a dry-goods store, or any other."

This was undoubtedly true. Work of any kind had no charms for Roswell. To walk up the avenue swinging a dandy cane, dressed in the height of the fashion, or, what was better yet, sitting back luxuriously in an elegant carriage drawn by a dashing span; such was what he regarded himself most fit for. But, unfortunately, he was not very likely to realize his wishes. The desire to enjoy wealth doesn't bring it, and the tastes of a gentleman are not a very good stock to begin life with. So Roswell sauntered along in rather a discontented frame of mind until he reached Madison Park, where he sat down on a bench, and listlessly watched some boys who were playing there.

"Hallo, Roswell!" said one of his acquaintances, coming up by chance. "How do you happen to be here?"

"Why shouldn't I be here?"

"I thought you were in a store somewhere on Sixth Avenue."

"Well, I was, but I have left it."

"When did you leave it?"

"To-day."

"Got sacked, hey?"

"Sacked," in the New York vernacular, means discharged from a place. The idea of having it supposed that he had been "sacked" was not pleasing to Roswell's pride. He accordingly answered, "I never was 'sacked' in my life. Besides, it's a low word, and I never use it."

"Well, you know what I mean. Did they turn you off?"

"No, they didn't. They would have been glad to have me stay."

"Why didn't you then?"

"I didn't like the business."

"Dry goods,—wasn't it?"

"Yes, a retail dry-goods store. If I ever go into that line again, it'll be in a wholesale store. There's a chance there for a man to rise."

"You don't call yourself a man yet,—do you?"

"I call myself a gentleman," said Roswell, shortly.

"What are you going to do now?"

"I'm in no hurry about a new place. I shall look round a little."

"Well, success to you. I must be getting back to the shop."

"What are you doing?"

"I'm learning a trade."

"Oh!" said Roswell, turning up his nose slightly, which was quite easy for him to do, as nature had given that organ an upward turn. He thought all trades low, and resolved hereafter to hold as little communication as possible with the boy who had so far demeaned himself as to be learning one. That was worse than being in a dry-goods store, and carrying around bundles.

Towards six o'clock Roswell rose from his seat, and sauntered towards Clinton Place, which was nearly a mile distant. He entered the house a little before dinner.

"Are you not earlier than usual, Roswell?" asked his mother.

"I've left the store," he said, abruptly.

"Left the store!" echoed his mother, in some dismay. "Why?"

"Because they don't know how to treat me. It's no fit place for a gentleman's son."

"I am sorry, Roswell," said Mrs. Crawford, who, like her son, was "poor and proud," and found the four dollars he earned weekly of advantage. "I'm afraid you have been foolish."

"Listen, mother, and I'll tell you all about it," he said.

Roswell gave his explanation, which, it need hardly be said, was very favorable to himself, and Mrs. Crawford was finally brought to believe that Hall & Turner were low people, with whom it was not suitable for one of her son's gentlemanly tastes to be placed. His vindication was scarcely over, when the bell rang, and his Cousin Gilbert was admitted.

Mr. Gilbert entered briskly, and with a smiling face. He felt unusually complaisant, having succeeded in his designs against our hero.

"Well, James," said Mrs. Crawford, "you look in better spirits than I feel."

"What's happened amiss?"

"Roswell has given up his place."

"Been discharged, you mean."

"No," said Roswell, "I left the place of my own accord."

"What for?"

"I don't like the firm, nor the business. I wish I were in Mr. Rockwell's."

"Well," said Gilbert, "perhaps I can get you in there."

"Has the boot-black left?"

"He's found another place," said Gilbert, smiling at what he regarded as a good joke.

"You don't mean to say he has left a place where he was earning ten dollars a week?" said Mrs. Crawford, in surprise. "Where is this new place that you speak of?"

"In the station-house."

"Is he in the station-house?" asked Roswell, eagerly.

"That is what I hear."

"What's he been doing?"

"Charged with picking a pocket."

"Well, I do hope Mr. Rockwell will now see his folly in engaging a boy from the streets," said Mrs. Crawford, charitably concluding that there was no doubt of our hero's guilt.

"What'll be done with him, Cousin James?" asked Roswell.

"He'll be sent to the Island, I suppose."

"He may get clear."

"I think not. Circumstances are very much against him, I hear."

"And will you try to get me in, Cousin James?"

"I'll do what I can. Perhaps it may be well for you to drop in to-morrow about ten o'clock."

"All right,—I'll do it."

Both Mrs. Crawford's and Roswell's spirits revived wonderfully, and Mr. Gilbert, too, seemed unusually lively. And all because poor Dick had got into difficulties, and seemed in danger of losing both his place and his good name.

"It's lucky I left Hall & Turner's just as I did!" thought Roswell, complacently. "May be they'd like to engage the boot-black when he gets out of prison. But I guess he'll have to go back to blacking boots. That's what he's most fit for."

CHAPTER XVII.

DICK'S ACQUITTAL.

After his interview with Mr. Murdock and Henry Fosdick, Dick felt considerably relieved. He not only saw that his friends were convinced of his innocence, but, through Tim Ryan's testimony, he saw that there was a reasonable chance of getting clear. He had begun to set a high value on respectability, and he felt that now he had a character to sustain.

The night wore away at last. The pallet on which he lay was rather hard; but Dick had so often slept in places less comfortable that he cared little for that. When he woke up, he did not at first remember where he was, but he very soon recalled the circumstances, and that his trial was close at hand.

"I hope Mr. Murdock won't oversleep himself," thought our hero. "If he does, it'll be a gone case with me."

At an early hour the attendant of the police station went the rounds, and Dick was informed that he was wanted. Brief space was given for the arrangement of the toilet. In fact, those who avail themselves of the free lodgings provided at the station-house rarely pay very great attention to their dress or personal appearance. Dick, however, had a comb in his pocket, and carefully combed his hair. He also brushed off his coat as well as he could; he also critically inspected his shoes, not forgetting his old professional habits.

"I wish I had a brush and some blackin'," he said to himself. "My shoes would look all the better for a good shine."

But time was up, and, under the escort of a policeman, Dick was conveyed to the Tombs. Probably all my readers have heard of this building. It is a large stone building, with massive columns, broad on the ground, but low. It is not only used for a prison, but there are two rooms on the first floor used for the holding of courts. Into the larger one of these Dick was carried. He looked around him anxiously, and to his great joy perceived that not only Mr. Murdock was on hand, but honest Tim Ryan, whose testimony was so important to his defence. Dick was taken forward to the place provided for those awaiting trial, and was obliged to await his turn. One or two cases, about which there was no doubt, including the colored woman arrested for drunkenness, were summarily disposed of, and the next case was called. The policeman who had arrested Dick presented himself with our hero.

Dick was so neatly dressed, and looked so modest and self-possessed, that the judge surveyed him with some surprise.

"What is this lad charged with?" he demanded.

"With taking a wallet from a gentleman's pocket," said the policeman.

"Did you arrest him?"

"I did."

"Did you take him in the act?"

"No; I did not see him take it."

"What have you to say, prisoner? Are you guilty or not guilty?" said the judge, turning to Dick.

"Not guilty," said Dick, quietly.

"State why you made the arrest," said the judge.

"I saw him with the wallet in his hand."

"Is the gentleman who had his pocket picked, present?"

"He is."

"Summon him."

The red-faced man came forward, and gave his testimony. He stated that he was standing on the sidewalk, when he felt a hand thrust into his pocket, and forcibly

69

withdrawn. He immediately felt for his wallet, and found it gone. Turning, he saw a boy running, and immediately gave chase.

"Was the boy you saw running the prisoner?"

"I suppose it was."

"You suppose? Don't you know?"

"Of course it was, or he would not have been found with the wallet in his hand."

"But you cannot identify him from personal observation?"

The red-faced man admitted with some reluctance that his eyesight was very poor, and he did not catch sight of the boy till he was too far off to be identified.

"This is not so clear as it might be," said the judge. "Still, appearances are against the prisoner, and as the wallet was found in his possession, he must be found guilty, unless that fact can be satisfactorily explained."

"I have a witness who can explain it," said Dick.

"Where is he?"

Tim Ryan, who understood that his evidence was now wanted, came forward.

After being sworn, the judge asked, "What is your name?"

"Tim Ryan, sir."

"Where do you live?"

"In Mulberry Street."

"Tell what you know of this case."

"I was standing in Chatham Street, when I saw the ould gintleman with the red face (here the prosecutor scowled at Tim, not relishing the description which was given of him) standing at the corner of Pearl Street. A boy came up, and put his hand into his pocket, and then run away as fast as his legs could carry him, wid the wallet in his hand."

"Who was this boy? Do you know him?"

"Yes, sir."

"Tell his name."

"It was Micky Maguire," said Tim, reluctantly.

"And who is Micky Maguire?"

"He blacks boots."

"Then if this Micky Maguire took the wallet, how happened it that it was found in this boy's possession?"

"I can tell that," said Tim. "I ran after Micky to see if he'd get off wid the wallet. He hadn't gone but a little way when I saw him slip it into Dick's pocket."

"I suppose you mean by Dick, the prisoner at the bar?"

"Yes, sir."

"And what became of this Micky?"

"He stopped runnin' after he'd got rid of the pocket-book, and a minute after, up came the 'copp,' and took Dick."

"Why didn't you come forward, and explain the mistake?"

"I was afraid Micky'd beat me."

"Do you know this Micky Maguire?" said the judge, turning to the officer.

"I do."

"What is his reputation?"

"Bad. He's been at the Island three or four times already."

"Did you see him anywhere about when you made the arrest?"

"I did."

"Do you know this boy who has just testified?"

"Yes. He is a good boy."

"The case seems a clear one. The prisoner is discharged from custody. Arrest Micky Maguire on the same charge as early as possible."

The next case was called, and Dick was free.

Mr. Murdock came forward, and took him by the hand, which he shook heartily.

"I congratulate you on your acquittal," he said.

"I feel a little better than I did," said Dick. "Tim, you're a good fellow," he said, clasping Tim's hand. "I wouldn't have got off, if it hadn't been for you."

"I ought to do that much for you, Dick, when you've been so kind to me."

"How are you getting along now, Tim?"

"Pretty well. Mother's got so she can work and we're doin' well. When she was sick, it was pretty hard."

"Here's something to help you along," said Dick, and he drew a bill from his pocket.

"Five dollars!" said Tim, in surprise.

"You can buy some new clothes, Tim."

"I ought not to take so much as that, Dick."

"It's all right, Tim. There's some more where that comes from."

They were in Centre Street by this time. Fosdick came up hurriedly.

"Have you got off, Dick?" he asked, eagerly.

"Yes, Fosdick. There's no chance of my being entertained at the expense of the city."

"I didn't expect the trial was coming off so early. Tell me all about it."

"What did they say at the house at my being away?" asked Dick.

"Miss Peyton inquired particularly after you. I said, as you directed me, that you were detained by important business."

"What did she say then?"

Dick was so particular in his inquiries, fearing lest any suspicion should have been formed of the real cause which had detained him. There was no reason for it; but it had always been a matter of pride with him in his vagabond days that he had never been arrested on any charge, and it troubled him that he should even have been suspected of theft.

"You are fishing for compliments, Dick," said Fosdick.

"How do you make that out?"

"You want to know what Miss Peyton said. I believe you are getting interested in her."

"When I am, just send me to a lunatic asylum," said Dick.

"I am afraid you are getting sarcastic, Dick. However, not to keep you in suspense, Miss Peyton said that you were one of the wittiest young men she knew of, and you were quite the life of the house."

"I suppose I ought to blush," said Dick; "but I'm a prey to hunger just now, and it's too much of an effort."

"I'll excuse you this time," said Fosdick. "As to the hunger, that's easily remedied. We shall get home to breakfast, and be in good time too."

Fosdick was right. They were the first to seat themselves at the table. Mr. Clifton came in directly afterwards. Dick felt a momentary embarrassment.

"What would he say," thought our hero, "if he knew where I passed the night?"

"Good-morning, Hunter," said Clifton. "You didn't favor us with your presence at dinner last evening."

"No," said Dick. "I was absent on very important business."

"Dining with your friend, the mayor, probably?"

"Well, no, not exactly," said Dick, "but I had some business with the city government."

"It seems to me that you're getting to be quite an important character."

"Thank you," said Dick. "I am glad to find that genius is sometimes appreciated."

Here Miss Peyton entered.

"Welcome, Mr. Hunter," she said. "We missed you last evening."

"I hope it didn't affect your appetite much," said Dick.

"But it did. I appeal to Mr. Fosdick whether I ate anything to speak of."

"I thought Miss Peyton had a better appetite than usual," said Fosdick.

"That is too bad of you, Mr. Fosdick," said Miss Peyton. "I'm sure I didn't eat more than my canary bird."

"Just the way it affected me," said Dick. "It always improves my appetite to see you eat, Miss Peyton."

Miss Peyton looked as if she hardly knew whether to understand this remark as complimentary or otherwise.

That evening, at the dinner-table, Clifton drew a copy of the "Express" from his pocket, and said, "By Jove, Hunter, here's a capital joke on you! I'll read it. 'A boy, named Richard Hunter, was charged with picking a pocket on Chatham Street; but it appearing that the theft was committed by another party, he was released from custody.'"

Dick's heart beat a little quicker while this was being read, but he maintained his self-possession.

"Of course," said he, "that was the important business that detained me. But I hope you won't mention it, for the sake of my family."

"I'd make the young rascal change his name, if I were you," said Clifton, "if he's going to get into the Police record."

"I think I shall," said Dick, "or maybe I'll change my own. You couldn't mention a highly respectable name that I could take,—could you?"

"Clifton is the most respectable name I know of," said the young gentleman owning that name.

"If you'll make me your heir, perhaps I'll adopt it."

"I'll divide my debts with you, and give you the biggest half," said Clifton.

It is unnecessary to pursue the conversation. Dick found to his satisfaction that no one at the table suspected that he was the Richard Hunter referred to in the "Express."

CHAPTER XVIII.

THE CUP AND THE LIP.

While Dick's night preceding the trial was an anxious one, Gilbert and Roswell Crawford passed a pleasant evening, and slept soundly.

"Do you think Mr. Rockwell would be willing to give me the same wages he has paid to the boot-black?" he inquired with interest.

"Perhaps he won't take you at all."

"I think he ought to pay some attention to your recommendation," said Mrs. Crawford. "You ought to have some influence with him."

"Of course," said Gilbert, "I shall do what I can in the matter; but it's a pity Roswell can't give better references."

"He's never been with a decent employer yet. He's been very unlucky about his places," said Mrs. Crawford.

She might have added that his employers had considered themselves unfortunate in their engagement of her son; but, even if she had known it, she would have considered that they were prejudiced against him, and that they were in fault entirely.

"I will do what I can for him," continued Gilbert; "but I am very sure he won't get as much as ten dollars a week."

"I can earn as much as the boot-black, I should hope," said Roswell.

"He didn't earn ten dollars a week."

"He got it."

"That's a very different thing."

"Well, if I get it, I don't care if I don't earn it."

"That's true enough," said Gilbert, who did not in his heart set a very high estimate upon the services of his young cousin, and who, had the business been his own, would certainly not have engaged him at any price.

Roswell thought it best not to say any more, having on some previous occasions been greeted with remarks from his cousin which could not by any means be regarded as complimentary.

"Do you think I had better come in at ten o'clock, Cousin James?" inquired Roswell, as breakfast was over, and Gilbert prepared to go to the counting-room.

"Well, perhaps you may come a little earlier, say about half-past nine," said the book-keeper.

"All right," said Roswell.

Being rather sanguine, he made up his mind that he was going to have the place, and felt it difficult to keep his good fortune secret. Now, in the next house there lived a boy named Edward McLean, who was in a broker's office in Wall Street, at a salary of six dollars a week. Now, though Edward had never boasted of his good fortune, it used to disturb Roswell to think that his place and salary were so much superior to his own. He felt that it was much more respectable to be in a broker's office, independent of the salary, than to run around the city with heavy bundles. But if he could enter such an establishment as Rockwell & Cooper's, at a salary of ten dollars, he felt that he could look down with conscious superiority upon Edward McLean, with his six dollars a week.

He went over to his neighbor's, and found Edward just starting for Wall Street.

"How are you, Roswell?" said Edward.

"Pretty well. Are you going down to the office?"

"Yes."

"You've got a pretty good place,—haven't you?"

"Yes, I like it."

"How much do you get?"

"Six dollars a week."

"That's very fair," said Roswell, patronizingly.

"How do you like your place?" asked Edward. "I believe you're in a dry-goods store on Sixth Avenue."

"Oh, no," said Roswell.

"You were?"

"Yes, I went in temporarily to oblige them," said Roswell, loftily; "but, of course, I wouldn't engage to remain any length of time in such a place, however large the inducements they might offer."

Considering Roswell's tone, it would hardly have been supposed that the large inducements were four dollars a week, and that, even at that compensation, his services were not desired.

"Then it wasn't a good place?" said Edward.

"Well enough for such as liked it," said Roswell. "I have no complaint of Hall & Turner. I told them that it was not dissatisfaction with them that led me to leave the place, but I preferred a different kind of business."

"Have you got another place?"

"I have an offer under consideration," said Roswell, consequentially; "one of the most solid firms in the city. They offer me ten dollars a week."

"Ten dollars a week!" repeated Edward, somewhat staggered by the statement. "That's big pay."

"Yes," said Roswell; "but I think I ought to get as much as that."

"Why, I thought myself lucky to get six dollars," said Edward.

"Yes, that's very fair," said Roswell, condescendingly. "In fact, I've worked at that figure myself; but, of course, one expects more as he grows older."

"I suppose you'll accept your offer," said Edward.

"I haven't quite made up my mind," said Roswell, carelessly. "I think I shall."

74

"You'd better. Such places don't grow on every bush."

Though Edward did not more than half believe Roswell's statement, he kept his disbelief to himself, feeling that it was a matter of indifference to him whether Roswell received a large or small salary.

"I must be going down to the office," he said. "Good-morning."

"Good-morning," said Roswell, and he re-entered the house, feeling that he had impressed Edward with a conviction of his superiority, and the value set upon his services by the business men of New York. He went upstairs, and picked out a flashy necktie from his drawer, tied it carefully before the glass, and about nine set out for Rockwell & Cooper's warehouse.

It is necessary for us to precede him.

Gilbert reached the counting-room at the usual time. His thoughts on the way thither were pleasant.

"I shan't be subjected to that young rascal's impertinence," he considered. "That's one satisfaction."

His astonishment, nay, dismay, may be imagined, therefore, when, on entering the counting-room, the first object his eyes rested on was the figure of Dick.

"Good-morning, Mr. Gilbert," said our hero, pleasantly.

"How came you here?" he demanded.

"I walked," said Dick. "I don't often ride. I think walkin's good for the constitution."

"You know what I mean, well enough. How did you get out of prison?"

"I haven't been there."

"You were arrested for picking a man's pocket yesterday afternoon," said Gilbert.

"Excuse me, Mr. Gilbert, you're slightly mistaken there. I was arrested *on suspicion* of picking a man's pocket."

"The same thing."

"Not quite, as it has been proved that I was innocent, and the wallet was taken by another boy."

"Have you been tried?"

"Yes, and acquitted."

Gilbert looked and felt disappointed. He could not conceive how Dick could have escaped when the plot to entrap him had been so artfully contrived.

"Well, young man," he said, "I'll give you a piece of advice, and if you're wise you'll follow it."

"That's kind in you," said Dick.

"I pass over your impertinence this time, and will advise you as a friend to resign your situation before Mr. Rockwell comes."

"Why should I?"

"It'll save your being discharged."

"Do you think he'll discharge me?"

"I know he will. He won't have any one in his employ who has been arrested for picking pockets."

"Not even if he didn't do it?"

"Not even if he was lucky enough to get off," said Gilbert.

"You think I'd better give up my place?"

"That'll be the best course for you to pursue."

"But how'll I get another place?"

"I'll do what I can to help you to another place if you leave at once."

"I think I'll wait and see Mr. Rockwell first."

"I'll make all the necessary explanations to Mr. Rockwell," said the book-keeper.

"I think I'd rather see him myself, if it doesn't make any difference to you."

"You're acting like a fool. You'll only be kicked out of the store. If you don't follow my advice, I shan't interest myself in getting you another place."

"Do you think I took the wallet, Mr. Gilbert?" asked Dick.

"Of course I do."

"Then how could you recommend me to another place?"

"Because I think this may prove a lesson to you. You've been lucky enough to escape this time, but you can't expect it always."

"I'm much obliged to you for your favorable opinion; but I don't think I shall resign at once."

At this moment Mr. Rockwell entered the warehouse. He had been informed of Dick's misfortune by Mr. Murdock, who had had occasion to call at his house on his way from the trial.

"How's this, Richard?" he said, advancing, with a frank smile. "I hear you got into strange quarters last night."

"Yes," said Dick; "but I didn't like it well enough to stay long."

"Why didn't you send for me?"

"Thank you, sir, I didn't like to trouble you. Mr. Murdock was very kind."

"Have they got the real thief?"

"I don't know, sir."

"Well, 'all's well that ends well.' You can afford to laugh at it now."

Mr. Gilbert listened to this colloquy with very little satisfaction.

It seemed to show such a good understanding between Dick and his employer that he perceived that it would be a very difficult thing to supersede him.

"Mr. Rockwell seems to be infatuated with that boy," he muttered to himself.

"I think I won't resign just yet," said Dick, in a low voice, to the book-keeper.

"You'll be found out some day," said Gilbert, snappishly. "Go to the post-office, and mind you don't stop to play on the way."

Dick started on his errand, and, in passing out into the street, encountered Roswell Crawford, who, attired with extra care, had just come down the street from Broadway. On seeing Dick, he started as if he had seen a ghost.

"Good-morning, Roswell," said Dick, pleasantly.

"Good-morning," said Roswell, stiffly.

"Your cousin is in the counting-room. I am in a hurry, and must leave you."

"I thought he was on his way to the Island by this time," thought Roswell, perplexed. "What can it mean?"

It occurred to him all at once that Dick might just have been discharged, and this thought cheered him up considerably. He entered the counting-room with a jaunty step.

"Good-morning, Cousin James," he said.

Gilbert turned round, and said, in a surly tone, "You may as well take yourself off. There's no chance for you here."

"Hasn't the boot-black been discharged?"

"No; and isn't going to be."

"How is that?" asked Roswell, looking very much disappointed.

"I can't stop to tell you now. You'd better go now, and I'll tell you this evening."

"Just my luck!" said Roswell to himself, considerably crest-fallen. "I wish I hadn't said a word to Edward McLean about the place."

CHAPTER XIX.

ANOTHER ARREST.

Micky Maguire, as the reader will remember, was by no means satisfied with the compensation he received from Gilbert for his share in the plot which came so near proving disastrous to our friend Dick.

He felt that the book-keeper had acted meanly to him, and he meant to have his revenge if a good opportunity should ever offer. He was very much disappointed to think he must do without the watch which he had set his heart upon. He would have felt no particular scruples against stealing it, but that would be rather dangerous. He began to wish he had kept the pocket-book. Very probably it contained more than enough to buy the watch.

But, in spite of his disappointment, he had one satisfaction. He had avenged himself upon Dick, whom he had long disliked. He knew nothing of Tim Ryan's testimony, and supposed there was no doubt of Dick's conviction. He would like very well to have been present at the trial; but he had unpleasant associations connected with the court-room at the Tombs, having figured there on several occasions in an important but not very enviable capacity.

As he was standing by the park railings, his particular friend and admirer, Limpy Jim, came up.

"Mornin', Jim," said Micky. "What luck?"

"None at all," said Jim. "I haven't had a shine yet, and I'm precious hungry."

"Come and take breakfast with me," said Micky, in an unusual fit of generosity; for he was generally more willing to be treated than to treat.

"Have you got stamps enough?"

"Look at this," and Micky displayed the bill which he had received from Gilbert.

"You're in luck, Micky. Did you make all that by shines?"

"Never mind how I made it. I guess it's good. Come along if you're hungry."

Limpy Jim followed Micky across Printing-House Square to a cheap restaurant on Nassau Street, between Ann and Beekman Streets, and they were soon partaking with relish of a breakfast which, as they were not very fastidious, proved abundantly satisfactory.

"I've got some news," said Micky, after he had drained his cup of coffee. "You haven't forgot Ragged Dick, have ye?"

"He's set up for a gentleman. I saw him a week ago strutting round as if he lived on Fifth Avenue."

"Well, he's set up for something else now."

"What's that?"

"A pick-pocket."

"What?" asked Jim, amazed.

"He stole an old chap's pocket-book yesterday afternoon, and I seed a policeman haulin' him off to the p'lice station."

"That's where he gets his good clo'es from?" suggested Jim.

"Most likely. I expect he's on his way to the Island by this time."

"Serve him right for puttin' on airs. He won't pretend to be so much better than the rest of us now."

"Wonder what Tom Wilkins'll say? He's a great friend of Dick's."

"He's a sneak," said Micky.

"That's so. I wanted to borrer a shillin' of him last week, and he wouldn't lend it to me."

This Tom Wilkins was a boot-black like the two who were expressing so unfavorable an opinion of his character. He had a mother and two sisters partially dependent upon him for support, and faithfully carried home all his earnings. This accounts for his being unwilling to lend Limpy Jim, who had no one to look out for but himself, and never considered it necessary to repay borrowed money. Tom had reason to feel friendly to Dick, for on several occasions, one of which is mentioned in the first volume of this series, Dick had given him help in time of need. He was always ready to defend Dick, when reviled by Micky and his followers, and had once or twice been attacked in consequence. Limpy Jim was right in supposing that nothing would disturb Tom more than to hear that his friend had got into trouble.

Micky, who was in a generous mood, bought a couple of cheap cigars, of which he presented one to his satellite. These were lighted, and both boys, feeling more comfortable for the hearty meal of which they had partaken, swaggered out into the street.

They re-entered the park, and began to look out for patrons.

"There's Tom Wilkins now," said Limpy Jim.

Tom was busily engaged in imparting a scientific shine to the boots of an old gentleman who was sitting on one of the wooden seats to be found in the neighborhood of the City Hall.

When he had completed his task, and risen from his knees, Limpy Jim advanced towards him, and said, with a sneer, "I've heard fine news about your friend Dick."

"What's that?" asked Tom.

"He's got nabbed by a 'copp.'"

"I don't believe it," said Tom, incredulously.

"Isn't it so, Micky?" said Jim, appealing to his friend.

"Yes, it's true. I seed him hauled off for pickin' an old fellow's pocket in Chatham Street."

"I don't believe it," repeated Tom; but he began to feel a little uneasy. "I saw him and spoke to him yesterday mornin'."

"What if you did? It didn't happen till afternoon."

"Dick wouldn't steal," said Tom, stoutly.

"He'll find it mighty hard work provin' that he didn't," said Micky. "You won't see him for the next three months."

"Why won't I?"

"Because he'll be at the Island. Maybe you'll go there yourself."

"If I do, it'll be for the first time," retorted Tom; "and that's more than either of you can say."

As this happened to be true, it was of course regarded as offensive.

"Shut up, Tom Wilkins!" said Micky, "if you don't want a lickin'."

"None of your impudence!" said Limpy Jim, emboldened by the presence and support of Micky, who was taller and stronger than Tom.

"I've only told the truth," said Tom, "and you can't deny it."

"Take that for your impudence!" said Micky, drawing off, and hitting Tom a staggering blow on the side of the head.

Limpy Jim was about to assist Micky, when there was a very unlooked-for interruption. Micky Maguire was seized by the collar, and, turning indignantly, found himself in the grip of a policeman.

"So you are fighting, are you, my fine fellow?" demanded the guardian of the public peace.

"He insulted me," said Micky, doggedly, not attempting resistance, which he knew would be ineffectual. "Didn't he, Jim?"

But Jim had already disappeared. He had a prejudice, easily accounted for, against the metropolitan police, and had as little communication with them as possible.

"I don't know anything about that," said the policeman. "All I know is that you're wanted."

"Just for hittin' him? I didn't hurt him any."

"He didn't hurt me much," said Tom, generously, not desiring to see Micky get into trouble on his account.

"He says I didn't hurt him," urged Micky. "Can't you let me go?"

"That isn't what I want you for," said the policeman.

Micky was astonished. The real cause of his arrest never once occurred to him, and he could not understand why he was "wanted."

"What is it, then?" he asked in some surprise. "What 'ave I been doin'?"

"Perhaps you don't remember relieving an old gentleman of his pocket-book yesterday in Chatham Street."

"'Twasn't me."

"Who was it then?"

"Ragged Dick,—the feller that was took at the time. I seed him pick the man's pocket."

"It seems that you remember something about it."

"But it was Dick that did it. If he says I did it, he lies."

"I've nothing to do with that. You must tell your story to the judge."

"Has he let Dick go?"

"Yes."

Micky received this intelligence with dismay. Somehow it had got out that he was the real thief, and he began to think that his chance of getting off was small. Just then, while in custody of the policeman, he saw advancing towards him the man who had inveigled him into the plot,—Gilbert, the book-keeper. His anger against Gilbert overcame his prudence, and he said, "Well, if I did take the pocket-book, I was paid for doin' it, and that was the man that hired me."

With some surprise, the policeman listened to this story.

"If you don't believe me, just wait till I speak to him."

"Mr. Gilbert!" called Micky.

Gilbert, who had not till now noticed his confederate, looked up, and, rapidly understanding what had happened, determined upon his course.

"Who speaks to me?" he said, quietly.

"You've got me into trouble, Mr. Gilbert," said Micky, "and I want you to get me out of it."

"What does he mean?" asked Gilbert, coolly, addressing the policeman.

"You hired me to steal a man's pocket-book, and I'm took up for it," said Micky. "I want you to help me, or I'll be sent to the Island."

"The boy must be crazy," said Gilbert, shrugging his shoulders.

"You give me a dollar to do it," said Micky, very much incensed at the desertion of his confederate.

"Do you know the boy?" asked the policeman respectfully, for he put no faith in Micky's statement.

"He blacked my boots once," said Gilbert. "That's all I know about him. What is he arrested for?"

"For picking pockets. There was another boy arrested on suspicion, but it appeared on trial that he was innocent, and that this boy really took the wallet."

"He looks like a young scamp," said Gilbert, coolly. "I'm much obliged to him for introducing my name into the matter. I hope he'll get his desserts."

This was too much for Micky's patience. He assailed Gilbert with such a shower of oaths that the policeman tightened his grip, and shook him vigorously. Gilbert shrugged his shoulders, and walked off with apparent unconcern.

"Wait till I get free," said Micky, furiously. "I'll fix him."

In regard to Micky, I have only to say further at this time, that he was at once conveyed to the Tombs, summarily tried and convicted, and spent the same night on Blackwell's Island, where we leave him for three months.

CHAPTER XX.

BEFORE THE PARTY.

"You'll be able to attend Ida Greyson's party after all, Dick," said Fosdick, on Tuesday evening.

"Yes," said Dick, "I was afraid that I should be wanted to grace the fashionable circles at Blackwell's Island; but as my particular friend Micky Maguire has kindly offered to go in my place, I shall be able to keep my other engagement."

"Micky's a bad fellow."

"I'm afraid he is," said Dick; "but he's never had a fair chance. His father was a drunkard, and used to beat him and his mother, till Micky ran away from home, and set up for himself. He's never had any good example set him."

"You speak kindly of Micky, considering he has always been your enemy."

"I haven't any ill will against Micky," said Dick, generously. "If I ever can do him a good turn I will. I've been luckier than he and most of my old companions, I'm going to do all I can to help them along. There's good in them if you can only bring it out."

Dick spoke earnestly, in a very different tone from his usual one. He had a certain philosophy of his own, and had always taken the world easily, however it treated him; but he had a warm and sympathizing heart for the sufferings of others, and he felt that he was in a position to befriend his old associates, and encourage them to higher aims and a better mode of life.

"You're a good fellow, Dick," said Fosdick. "It isn't everybody that is so charitable to the faults of others."

"I know one," said Dick, smiling.

"You mean me; but I'm afraid you are mistaken. I can't say I feel very well disposed towards Micky Maguire."

"Maybe Micky'll reform and turn out well after all."

"It would be a wonderful change."

"Haven't both of us changed wonderfully in the last eighteen months?"

"You were always a good fellow, even when you were Ragged Dick."

"You say that because you are my friend, Fosdick."

"I say it because it's true, Dick. You were always ready to take the side of the weak against the strong, and share your money with those who were out of luck. I had a hard time till I fell in with you."

"Thank you," said Dick; "if I ever want a first-rate recommendation I'll come to you. What a lot of friends I've got! Mr. Gilbert offered to get me another place if I'd only resign my situation at Rockwell & Cooper's."

"He's a very disinterested friend," said Fosdick, laughing. "Do you think of accepting his offer?"

"I'm afraid I might not be suited with the place he'd get me," said Dick. "He thinks I'm best fitted to adorn the office of a boot-black. Maybe he'd appoint me his private boot-black; but I'm afraid I shouldn't be able to retire on a fortune till I was two or three hundred, if I accepted the situation."

"What shall we wear to the party, Dick?"

"We've got good suits of clothes. We can carry them to a tailor's and have them pressed, and they will look well enough. I saw a splendid necktie to-day at a store on Broadway. I'm going to buy it."

"You have a weakness for neckties, Dick."

"You see, Fosdick, if you have a striking necktie, people will look at that, and they won't criticise your face."

"There may be something in that, Dick. I feel a little nervous though. It is the first fashionable party I ever attended."

"Well," said Dick, "I haven't attended many. When I was a boot-black I found it interfered with my business, and so I always declined all the fashionable invitations I got."

"You'd have made a sensation," said Fosdick, "if you had appeared in the costume you then wore."

"That's what I was afraid of. I don't want to make a sensation. I'm too modest."

In fact both the boys, though they were flattered by Ida's invitation, looked forward rather nervously to the evening of the party. For the first time they were to meet and mingle on terms of equality with a large number of young people who had been brought up very differently from themselves. Dick could not help remembering how short a time had elapsed since, with his little wooden box strapped to his back, he used to call out, "Black your boots?" in the city park. Perhaps some of his old customers might be present. Still he knew that he had improved greatly, and that his appearance had changed for the better. It was hardly likely that any one seeing him in Mr. Greyson's drawing-room, would identify him as the Ragged Dick of other days. Then there was another ground for confidence. Ida liked him, and he had a sincere liking for the little girl for whom he had a feeling such as a brother has for a cherished younger sister. So Dick dressed himself for the party, feeling that he should "get through it somehow."

I need not say, of course, that his boots shone with a lustre not to be surpassed even by the professional expert of the Fifth Avenue Hotel. It was very evident that Dick had not forgotten the business by which he once gained his livelihood.

When Dick had arranged his necktie to suit him, which I am bound to confess took at least quarter of an hour, had carefully brushed his hair, and dusted his clothes, he certainly looked remarkably well. Dick was not vain, but he was anxious to appear to advantage on his first appearance in society. It need not be added that Fosdick also was neatly dressed, but he was smaller and more delicate-looking than Dick, and not likely to attract so much attention.

As the boys were descending the stairs they met Miss Peyton.

"Really, Mr. Hunter," said that young lady, "you look quite dazzling this evening. How many hearts do you expect to break this evening?"

"I'm not in that line of business," said Dick. "I leave all that to you."

"You're too bad, really, Mr. Hunter," said Miss Peyton, highly pleased, nevertheless. "I never think of such a thing."

"I suppose I must believe you," said Dick, "but why is it that Mr. Clifton has looked so sad lately?"

"Mr. Clifton would not think of poor me," said Miss Peyton.

"If you only knew what he said about you the other day."

"Do tell me."

"I couldn't."

"If you will, I'll give you—"

"Thank you," interrupted Dick, gravely; "but I never accept kisses from ladies over six years old."

"How can you say so, Mr. Hunter?"

"I'm sorry to disappoint you, Miss Peyton, but I really couldn't."

"As if I ever thought of such a thing!" said Miss Peyton, in affected horror.

"I appeal to my friend Fosdick."

"Did I say so, Mr. Fosdick?"

Fosdick smiled.

"You mustn't appeal to me, Miss Peyton. You and Mr. Hunter are so brilliant that I don't pretend to understand you."

"Then you won't tell me what Mr. Clifton said. It is too bad. I shan't sleep to-night for thinking of it."

"Suppose you ask Mr. Clifton."

"I don't know but I will."

Miss Peyton went into the parlor, her heart fluttering with the thought that she had made a conquest of the gentleman referred to. As Mr. Clifton was a clerk on a small salary, continually in debt, and with no expectations, he could not be considered a very brilliant match; but Miss Peyton was not very particular, and she would have readily changed her name to Clifton if the chance should present itself. As we may not have occasion to refer to her again, it may be as well to state that Mr. Clifton's pecuniary affairs came to a crisis some months afterwards. He had always been in the habit of laughing at Miss Peyton; but in his strait he recollected that she was mistress of a few thousand dollars over which she had absolute control. Under these circumstances he decided to sacrifice himself. He accordingly offered his heart and hand, and was promptly accepted. Miss Peyton informed him that he was "the object of her heart's tenderest affection, her first and only love." Mr. Clifton expressed no doubt of this, though he was aware that Miss Peyton had been laying her snares for a husband for nearly ten years.

The marriage took place at the boarding-house, Dick and Fosdick being among the invited guests.

Mr. Clifton with his wife's money bought a partnership in a retail store on Eighth Avenue, where it is to be hoped he is doing a good business. Any one desirous of calling upon him at his place of business is referred to the New York City Directory for his number. Whether Mr. and Mrs. Clifton live happily I cannot pretend to say, not being included in the list of their friends; but I am informed by my friend Dick, who calls occasionally, that Mrs. Clifton is as fascinating now as before her marriage, and very naturally scorns the whole sisterhood of old maids, having narrowly escaped becoming one herself.

CHAPTER XXI.

IDA GREYSON'S PARTY.

When Dick and his friend reached Mr. Greyson's house, two carriages stood before the door, from each of which descended young guests, who, like themselves, had been invited to the party. One of these brought two young girls of twelve, the other two boys of twelve and fourteen, and their sister of ten. Entering with this party, the two boys felt less embarrassed than if they had been alone. The door was opened by a servant, who said, "Young ladies' dressing-room, second floor, left-hand room. Young gentlemen's dressing-room opposite."

Following directions, the boys went upstairs and entered a spacious chamber, where they deposited their outer garments, and had an opportunity to arrange their hair and brush their clothes.

"Is your sister here this evening?" asked one of the boys, addressing Dick.

"No," said Dick, soberly; "she couldn't come."

"I'm sorry for that. She promised to dance with me the first Lancers."

"Wouldn't I do as well?" asked Dick.

"I don't think you would," said the other, laughing. "But I'll tell you what,—you shall dance with my sister."

"I will, with pleasure," said Dick, "if you'll introduce me."

"Why, I thought you knew her," said the other, in surprise.

"Perhaps I did," said Dick; "but I exchanged myself off for another boy just before I came, and that makes a difference, you know. I shouldn't have known you, if you hadn't spoken to me."

"Do you know me now?" asked the other boy, beginning to understand that he had made a mistake.

"You live on Twenty-First Street,—don't you?"

"Yes," was the unexpected reply, for Dick had by a curious chance guessed right. "You're Henry Cameron, after all."

"No," said Dick; "my name is Richard Hunter."

"And mine is Theodore Selden; but I suppose you knew that, as you knew where I live. If you're ready, we'll go downstairs."

"Come, Fosdick," said Dick.

"We're going to have the Lancers first," said Theodore. "Ida told my sister so. Have you a partner engaged?"

"No."

"Then I'll introduce you to my sister. Come along."

I may explain here that Dick, and Fosdick also, had several times danced the Lancers in the parlor at the boarding-house in the evening, so that they felt reasonably confident of getting through respectably. Still his new friend's proposal made Dick feel a little nervous. He was not bashful with boys, but he had very little acquaintance with girls or young ladies, and expected to feel ill at ease with them. Still he could not think of a good reason for excusing himself from the promised introduction, and, after going up to Ida in company with his new friend, and congratulating her on her birthday (he would not have known how to act if Theodore had not set him an example), he walked across the room to where one of the young ladies who had entered at the time he did was seated.

"Alice," said Theodore, "this is my friend Mr. Hunter, who would like to dance with you in the first Lancers."

Dick bowed, and Alice, producing a card, said, "I shall be most happy. Will Mr. Hunter write his name on my card?"

Dick did so, and was thankful that he could now write a handsome hand.

"Now," said Theodore, unceremoniously, "I'll leave you two to amuse each other, while I go off in search of a partner."

"I'm in for it," thought Dick, seating himself on the sofa beside Alice. "I wish I knew what to say."

"Do you like the Lancers?" inquired the young lady.

"Yes, I like it," said Dick, "but I haven't danced it much. I'm afraid I shall make some mistakes."

"I've no doubt we shall get along well," said Alice. "Where did you learn?"

"I learned at home," said Dick.

"I thought I had not met you at Dodworth's. I attended dancing school there last winter."

"No," said Dick; "I never took lessons."

"Don't you like Ida Greyson?" inquired Alice.

"Yes, I like her very much," said Dick, sincerely.

"She's a sweet girl. She's a very intimate friend of mine. Who is that boy that came into the room with you?"

"His name is Henry Fosdick."

"He's going to dance with Ida. Come, let us hurry and get in the same set."

Dick offered his arm, and, as the sets were already being formed, led his partner to the upper end of the room, where they were just in time to get into the same set with Ida.

Theodore, with a girl about his own age, had already taken his position opposite Dick. Fosdick and Ida were the first couple, and opposite them Isaac and Isabella Selden, cousins of Theodore and Alice.

They had scarcely taken their places when the music struck up. Dick felt a little flustered, but determined to do his best. Being very quick in learning figures, and naturally gracefully in his movements, he got through very creditably, and without a mistake.

"I thought you expected to make mistakes," said Alice Selden, as Dick led her back to her seat. "I think you dance very well."

"It was because I had such a good partner," said Dick.

"Thank you for the compliment," said Alice, courtesying profoundly.

"Seems to me you're very polite, Alice," said Theodore, coming up.

"Mr. Hunter was paying me a compliment," said Alice.

"I wish you'd tell me how," said Theodore to Dick.

"I wish he would," interrupted Alice. "All your compliments are of the wrong kind."

"It isn't expected that brothers should compliment their sisters," said Theodore.

Mrs. Greyson came into the room during the dancing, and was pleased to see that Dick and Henry Fosdick, instead of sitting awkwardly in the corner, were taking their part in the evening's amusement. Dick made an engagement with Alice for another dance later in the evening, but danced the second with Ida Greyson, with whom, by this time, he felt very well acquainted.

"I didn't know you knew Alice Selden," said Ida. "Where did you meet her?"

"Her brother Theodore introduced me this evening. I did not know her before."

"You haven't been here lately, Dick," said Ida, familiarly.

"No," said he. "It's because I've been very busy."

"You don't work in the evening,—do you?"

"I study in the evening."

"What do you study, Dick?"

"French, for one thing."

"Can you speak French?"

"A little. Not much."

"I'm going to try you '*Comment vous portez-vous, monsieur?*'"

"'*Très bien, mademoiselle. Et vous?*'"

"That's right," said Ida, gravely. "I can't talk much yet myself. Who teaches you?"

"I have a private teacher."

"So have I. She comes twice a week. When I don't know my lesson, she boxes my ears. Is your teacher cross?"

"No," said Dick, laughing. "He doesn't box my ears."

"That's because you're so large. I wish I could have you for my teacher. I'd ask papa, if you could only speak it like a native."

"So I can," said Dick.

"You can, really?"

"Yes, like a native of New York."

Ida laughed, and was afraid that wouldn't do.

When the dance was over, and Dick was leading Ida to her seat, a surprise awaited him. A boy came forward hastily, and said in a tone blending amazement with gratification, "Is it possible that this is Dick Hunter?"

"Frank Whitney!" exclaimed Dick, clasping his hand cordially. "How came you here?"

"Just the question I was going to ask you, Dick. But I'll answer first. I am spending a few days with some cousins in Thirty-Seventh Street. They are friends of the Greysons, and were invited here this evening, and I with them. I little dreamed of meeting you here. I must say, Dick, you seem quite at home."

"Mr. Greyson has been a kind friend of mine," said Dick, "and I've met Ida quite often. But I felt a little nervous about coming to this party. I was afraid I'd be like a cat in a strange garret."

"You're a wonderful boy, Dick. You look as if you had been used to such scenes all your life. I can hardly believe you're the same boy I met in front of the Astor House a little more than a year ago."

"If I'm changed, it's because of what you said to me then, you and your father. But for those words I might still have been Ragged Dick."

"I'm glad to hear you say that, Dick; but, for all that, a great deal of credit is due to yourself."

"I've worked hard," said Dick, "because I felt that I had something to work for. When are you going to enter college?"

"I expect to apply for admission in about two months."

"At Columbia College?"

"Yes."

"I am glad of that. I shall hope to see you sometimes."

"You will see me often, Dick."

Here the music struck up, and the boys parted. It is unnecessary to speak farther of the events of the evening. Dick made several other acquaintances, and felt much more at ease than he had anticipated. He returned home, feeling that his first party had been a very agreeable one, and that he had on the whole appeared to advantage.

CHAPTER XXII.

MICKY MAGUIRE RETURNS FROM THE ISLAND.

For three months Micky Maguire was not seen in his accustomed haunts. During his involuntary residence at the Island he often brooded over the treachery of Gilbert, to whom his present misfortune was due. He felt that he had been selfishly left to his fate by his equally guilty confederate. It had certainly been a losing speculation for poor Micky. He had received but a paltry dollar for his services, and in return he was deprived of his liberty for three months.

The disgrace of being sent to the Island Micky did not feel as Dick would have done. He had been there too many times to care for that. But he did not like the restraints of the place, and he did like the free and independent life of the streets from which for a time he was debarred.

The result of Micky's brooding was a strong thirst for vengeance upon the author of his misfortunes. He could do nothing at present, but only bide his time.

Meanwhile things went on pretty much as usual at the establishment in Pearl Street. Gilbert liked Dick no better than he had done. In fact, he disliked him more, but, seeing the friendly relations between Dick and his employer, found it prudent to treat him well whenever Mr. Rockwell was by. At other times he indulged in sneers and fault-finding, which Dick turned off good-humoredly, or returned some droll answer, which blunted the edge of the sarcasm, and made the book-keeper chafe with the feeling that he was no match for the boy he hated. Dick, by faithful attention to his duties, and a ready comprehension of what was required of him, steadily advanced in the good opinion of every one except Gilbert.

"Keep on as you have begun, Richard," said Mr. Murdock to him, "and you'll be a member of the firm some time."

"Do you really think so, Mr. Murdock?" asked Dick, with a flush of gratification.

"I really do. You have excellent abilities, Mr. Rockwell likes you, and you have only to continue steady and faithful, and you'll be sure to rise."

"You know what I was, Mr. Murdock."

"You are none the worse for that, Richard. It is a great credit to a boy to earn his own living when circumstances force it upon him. If his employment is an honest one, it is an honorable one."

By such remarks as these Dick was encouraged, and he felt that Mr. Murdock was a true friend to him. Meanwhile a way was opening for his advancement.

One day Micky Maguire appeared in his old haunts. The second day he met Gilbert in the street; but the book-keeper took not the slightest notice of him. That touched Micky's pride, and confirmed him in his resolution. He decided to make known to Mr. Rockwell Gilbert's share in the little plot, thinking that this would probably be the best method of injuring him.

He ascertained, by means of a directory, with some difficulty, for Micky's education was rather slight, the residence of Mr. Rockwell, and about eight o'clock in the evening ascended the steps and rang the bell. He might have gone to his place of business, but Gilbert would be there, and he preferred to see Mr. Rockwell at home.

The servant stared at the odd and not particularly prepossessing figure before her.

"Is Mr. Rockwell at home?" asked Micky.

"Yes."

"I want to see him."

"Did he tell you to call?"

"It's on particular business," said Micky.

"Stop here and I'll tell him," said the girl.

"There's a boy at the door wants to see you, Mr. Rockwell," said the girl.

"Did you ask him in?"

"No sir. He looks like a suspicious carakter," said Bridget, laying the stress on the second syllable.

Mr. Rockwell rose, and went to the door.

"What is your business?" he asked.

"It's about Dick,—Ragged Dick we used to call him," said Micky.

"You mean Richard Hunter."

"Yes," said Micky. "He was took up for stealin' a gentleman's pocket-book three months ago."

"But he was proved innocent," said Mr. Rockwell, "so, if you have anything to say against him, your time is thrown away."

"I know he was innocent," said Micky; "another boy took it."

"Who was he?"

"I did it."

"Then you did a wicked thing in stealing the money, and a mean thing in trying to get an innocent boy into trouble."

"I wouldn't have done it," said Micky, "if I hadn't been paid for it."

"Paid for stealing!" said Mr. Rockwell, astonished.

"Paid for tryin' to get Dick into trouble."

"That does not seem to be a very likely story," said Mr. Rockwell. "Who would pay you money for doing such a thing?"

"Mr. Gilbert."

"My book-keeper?"

"Yes," said Micky, vindictively.

"I can hardly believe this," said Mr. Rockwell.

"He paid me only a dollar for what I did," said Micky, in an injured tone. "He'd ought to have given me five dollars. He's a reg'lar mean feller."

"And is this why you betray him now?"

"No," said Micky; "it isn't the money, though it's mean to expect a feller to run the risk of bein' nabbed for a dollar; but when the 'copp' had got hold of me I met him, and he said I was a young scamp, and he didn't know anything about me."

"Is this true?" asked Mr. Rockwell, looking keenly at Micky.

Micky confirmed his statement by an oath.

"I don't want you to swear. I shall not believe you the sooner for that. Can you explain why Mr. Gilbert should engage in such a base conspiracy?"

"He told me that he hated Dick," said Micky.

"Do you like him?"

"No, I don't," said Micky, honestly; "but I hate Mr. Gilbert worse."

"Why do you hate Richard?"

"Because he puts on airs."

"I suppose," said Mr. Rockwell, smiling, "that means that he wears good clothes, and keeps his face and hands clean."

"He wasn't nothin' but a boot-black," said Micky, in an injured tone.

"What are you?"

"I'm a boot-black too; but I don't put on airs."

"Do you mean to be a boot-black all your life?"

"I dunna," said Micky; "there aint anything else to do."

"Tell me truly, wouldn't you rather wear good clothes than poor ones, and keep yourself clean and neat?"

"Yes, I should," said Micky, after a slight hesitation.

"Then why do you blame Dick for preferring to do the same?"

"He licked me once," said Micky, rather reluctantly, shifting his ground.

"What for?"

"I fired a stone at him."

"You can't blame him much for that, can you?"

"No," said Micky, slowly, "I dunno as I can."

"For my own part I have a very good opinion of Richard," said Mr. Rockwell. "He wants to raise himself in the world, and I am glad to help him. If that is putting on airs, I should be glad to see you doing the same."

"There aint no chance for me," said Micky.

"Why not?"

"I aint lucky as Dick is."

"Dick may have been lucky," said Mr. Rockwell, "but I generally find that luck comes oftenest to those who deserve it. If you will try to raise yourself I will help you."

"Will you?" asked Micky, in surprise.

The fact was, he had been an Ishmaelite from his earliest years, and while he had been surrounded by fellows like Limpy Jim, who were ready to encourage and abet him in schemes of mischief, he had never had any friends who deserved the name. That a gentleman like Mr. Rockwell should voluntarily offer to assist him was indeed surprising.

"How old are you?" asked Mr. Rockwell.

"Seventeen," said Micky.

"How long have you blacked boots?"

"Ever since I was eight or nine."

"I think it is time for you to do something else."

"What will I do?"

"We must think of that. I must also think of the information you have given me in regard to Mr. Gilbert. You are certain you are telling the truth."

"Yes," said Micky; "it's the truth."

Micky did not swear this time, and Mr. Rockwell believed him.

"Let me see," he said, reflecting; "can you be at my store to-morrow morning at ten o'clock?"

"I can," said Micky, promptly.

"What is your name?"

"Micky Maguire."

"Good-night, Michael."

"Good-night, sir," said Micky, respectfully.

He walked away with a crowd of new thoughts and new aspirations kindling in his breast. A gentleman had actually offered to help him on in the world. Nobody had ever taken any interest in him before. Life to him had been a struggle and a conflict, with very little hope of better things. He had supposed he should leave off blacking boots some time, but no prospect seemed open before him.

"Why shouldn't I get up in the world?" he thought, with new ambition.

He half confessed to himself that he had led a bad life, and vague thoughts of amendment came to him. Somebody was going to take an interest in him. That was the secret of his better thoughts and purposes.

On the whole, I begin to think there is hope for Micky.

CHAPTER XXIII.

FAME AND FORTUNE.

Mr. Gilbert chanced to be looking out of the window of Mr. Rockwell's counting-room, when he was unpleasantly surprised by the sudden apparition of Micky Maguire. He was destined to be still more unpleasantly surprised. Micky walked up to the main entrance, and entered with an assured air. Gilbert hastened to meet him, and prevent his entrance.

"Clear out of here, you young rascal!" he said, in a tone of authority. "You're not wanted here."

"I've come on business," said Micky, with a scowl of dislike, showing no intention of retreating.

"I have no business with you," said Gilbert.

"Perhaps you haven't," said Micky, "but Mr. Rockwell has."

"Mr. Rockwell will have nothing to say to a vagabond like you."

"He told me to come," said Micky, resolutely, "and I shan't go till I've seen him."

Gilbert did not believe this, but suspected that Micky intended to betray him, and to this of course he had a decided objection.

"Go out!" he said, imperiously, "or I'll make you."

"I won't then," said Micky, defiantly.

"We'll see about that."

Gilbert seized him by the shoulders; but Micky was accustomed to fighting, and made a vigorous resistance. In the midst of the fracas Mr. Rockwell came up.

"What does this mean?" he demanded, in a quiet but authoritative tone.

"This young rascal has attempted to force his way in," said the book-keeper, desisting, and with a flushed face.

"I asked to see you," said Micky, "and he said I shouldn't."

"I told him to come," said Mr. Rockwell. "You may come into the counting-room, Michael. Mr. Gilbert, I should like your presence also."

In surprise, not unmingled with foreboding, Mr. Gilbert followed his employer and Micky Maguire into the counting-room.

"Mr. Gilbert," commenced Mr. Rockwell, "are you acquainted with this boy?"

"He blacked my boots on one occasion," said the book-keeper; "I know no more of him except that he is a young vagabond and a thief."

"Who hired me to steal?" retorted Micky.

"I don't think you would need any hiring," said Gilbert, with a sneer.

Micky was about to retort in no choice terms, but Mr. Rockwell signed to him to be silent.

"This boy has made a charge against you, Mr. Gilbert," he said, "which you ought to be made aware of."

"He is capable of any falsehood," said the book-keeper; but he began to be nervous.

"I thought your acquaintance with him was very slight."

"So it is; but it is easy to judge from his looks what he is."

"That is not always a safe guide. But to the charge. He asserts that you hired him to fix the charge of theft upon Richard, on account of your dislike to him."

"So he did, and all he give me was a dollar," said Micky, aggrieved. "That was mean."

"Do you believe this story?" asked Gilbert, turning to Mr. Rockwell.

"I know that you dislike Richard, Mr. Gilbert."

"So I do. He's artful and bad; but you'll find him out some day."

"I don't think you do him justice. Artful is the very last word I should apply to him."

"You may be deceived."

"If I am, I shall never put confidence in any boy again. But you haven't answered the charge, Mr. Gilbert."

"It isn't worth answering," said the book-keeper, scornfully.

"Still, I would be glad to have you give an answer one way or the other," persisted Mr. Rockwell.

"Then it's a lie, of course."

"It's true," said Micky.

"I hope you consider my word as of more value than this vagabond's," said Gilbert, contemptuously.

"Why were you so anxious to prevent his entering, Mr. Gilbert?"

"I didn't see what business he could possibly have here."

"Michael, will you give an account of all that has taken place between Mr. Gilbert and yourself? I do not yet feel satisfied."

"Mr. Rockwell," said Gilbert, in a passion, "I do not choose to submit to the insulting investigation you propose. My month is out next Thursday; I beg leave to resign my situation."

"Your resignation is accepted," said Mr. Rockwell, quietly.

"If it is convenient to you, I should like to leave at once," said the book-keeper, livid with passion.

"As you please," said his employer. "Your salary shall be paid up to the end of the month."

To this Gilbert offered no opposition. The balance of his salary was paid him, and he left the warehouse in a very unpleasant frame of mind, much to the gratification of Micky Maguire, who felt that his vengeance was complete.

"Now, Michael," said Mr. Rockwell, "I must see what I can do for you. Do you wish to give up your present business?"

"Yes," said Micky, "I don't like it."

"I can give you a situation as errand-boy in my own employ," said Mr. Rockwell. "My head clerk will explain your duties."

"What wages will I get?" asked Micky, anxiously.

"For the present you shall have a dollar a day, or six dollars a week. I will besides give you a new suit of clothes. Will that suit you?"

"Yes," said Micky, feeling as if he had unexpectedly become heir to a fortune. "When will I begin?"

"To-morrow if you like. Come here this afternoon at three, and I will send Richard with you to a clothing-house."

Just then Dick, who had been to the post-office, entered, and Mr. Rockwell in a few words informed him of the changes that had taken place.

"I believe you and Michael haven't been very good friends," he added; "but I trust you will get over that."

Dick promptly offered his hand to his old enemy.

"I am glad you are coming here, Micky," he said "I'll do all I can to help you on, and if we are not good friends it won't be my fault."

"Do you mean that, Dick?" said Micky, almost incredulous.

"Yes, I do."

"I've acted mean by you more'n once."

"If you have, it's all over now," said Dick. "There's no use in remembering it."

"You're a good fellow, Dick," said Micky, "an' I ought to have known it before."

Dick was gratified by this testimony from one who for years had been his active opponent, and he determined to help Micky to turn over the new leaf which was to bear a very different record from the old one.

When Micky had gone out, Mr. Rockwell said, "Well, Richard, I have lost my book-keeper."

"Yes, sir," said Dick.

"And I can't say I am sorry. I will do Mr. Gilbert the justice to say that he understood his business; but he was personally disagreeable, and I never liked him. Now I suppose I must look out for a successor."

"Yes, sir, I suppose so."

"I know a very competent book-keeper, who is intending to go into business for himself at the expiration of six months. Until that time I can secure his services. Now, I have a plan in view which I think you will approve. You shall at once commence the study of book-keeping in a commercial school in the evening, and during the day I will direct Mr. Haley to employ you as his assistant. I think in that way you will be able to succeed him at the end of his term."

Dick was completely taken by surprise. The thought that he, so recently plying the trade of a boot-black in the public streets, could rise in six months to the responsible post of a book-keeper in a large wholesale house, seemed almost incredible.

"I should like nothing better," he said, his eyes sparkling with delight, "if you really think I could discharge the duties satisfactorily."

"I think you could. I believe you have the ability, and of your fidelity I feel assured."

"Thank you, sir; you are very kind to me," said Dick, gratefully.

"I have reason to be," said Mr. Rockwell, taking his hand. "Under God it is to your courage that I owe the life of my dear boy. I shall never forget it. One thing more. I intend Michael to undertake most of your present duties, such as going to the post-office, etc. Do you think he will answer?"

"I think so," said Dick. "He has been a rough customer, but then he has never had a chance. I believe in giving everybody a chance."

"So do I," said Mr. Rockwell. "Michael shall have his chance. Let us hope he will improve it."

There are many boys, and men too, who, like Micky Maguire, have never had a fair chance in life. Let us remember that, when we judge them, and not be too hasty to condemn. Let us consider also whether it is not in our power to give some one the chance that may redeem him.

That afternoon Micky Maguire was provided with a new suit of clothes, of which he felt very proud. The next morning, on his way to the post-office, he fell in with his old confederate, Limpy Jim, who regarded him with a glance of the most bewildering surprise.

"It aint you, Micky,—is it?" he asked, cautiously, surveying his old comrade's neat appearance. "When did you come back from the Island?"

"Shut up about the Island, Jim," said Micky. "Do I look as if I had been there?"

"You look nobby," said Jim. "Where's your brush?"

"I've give up the blackin' business," said Micky.

"You have? What are you going to do? Sell papers?"

"No," said Micky, consequentially. "I'm in business on Pearl Street."

"Why," said Limpy Jim, surprised, "that's where that upstart Ragged Dick works."

"He aint an upstart, an' he aint ragged," said Micky. "He's a friend of mine, an' if you insult him, I'll lam' ye."

"O my eyes!" ejaculated Jim, opening the organs of vision to a very wide extent; "that's the biggest joke I ever heerd of."

"You'll hear of a bigger one pretty quick," said Micky, rolling up his sleeves, and squaring off scientifically.

Limpy Jim, who had a respect for Micky's prowess, incontinently fled, surveying Micky from a safe distance, with a look in which surprise seemed to mingle with incredulity.

It may seem strange, but, from that time forth, Dick had no firmer friend than Micky Maguire, who, I am glad to say, though occasionally wayward, improved vastly, and became a useful employé of the establishment which he had entered. Of course both in ability and education, though in the last he gained considerably, he was quite inferior to Dick; but he was advanced as he grew older to the position of porter, where his strength stood him in good stead. His pay increased also, and through Dick's influence he was saved from vicious habits, and converted from a vagabond to a useful member of society.

And now, almost with regret, I find myself closing up the record of Dick's chequered career. The past with its trials is over; the future expands before him, a bright vista of merited success. But it remains for me to justify the title of my story, and show how Dick acquired "Fame and Fortune." I can only hint briefly at the steps that led to them.

In six months, at the age of seventeen, Dick succeeded to Mr. Gilbert's place with a salary, to commence with, of one thousand dollars. To this an annual increase was made, making his income at twenty-one, fourteen hundred dollars. Just about that time he had an opportunity to sell his up-town lots, to a gentleman who had taken a great fancy to them, for five times the amount he paid, or five thousand dollars. His savings from his salary amounted to about two thousand dollars more.

Meanwhile Mr. Rockwell's partner, Mr. Cooper, from ill health felt obliged to withdraw from business, and Richard, to his unbounded astonishment and gratification, was admitted to the post of junior partner, embarking the capital he had already accumulated, and receiving a corresponding share of the profits. These were so large that Richard was able to increase his interest yearly by investing his additional savings, and three years later he felt justified in offering his hand to Ida Greyson, whose partiality to Dick had never wavered. He was no longer Ragged Dick now, but Mr. Richard Hunter, junior partner in the large firm of Rockwell & Hunter. Mr. Greyson felt that even in a worldly way Dick was a good match for his daughter; but he knew and valued still more his good heart and conscientious fidelity to duty, and excellent principles, and cheerfully gave his consent. Last week I read Dick's marriage in the papers, and rejoiced in his new hopes of happiness.

So Dick has achieved Fame and Fortune,—the fame of an honorable and enterprising man of business, and a fortune which promises to be very large. But I am glad to say that Dick has not been spoiled by prosperity. He never forgets his humble beginnings, and tries to show his sense of God's goodness by extending a helping hand to the poor and needy boys, whose trials and privations he understands well from his own past experience. I propose in my next story to give an account of one of these boys, and shall take the opportunity to give further information in regard to some of the characters introduced in this volume. This story, the third in the Ragged Dick series; will be entitled

Mark, the Match Boy;

or,

Richard Hunter's Ward.

Made in the USA
Columbia, SC
25 September 2023

23373691R00059